The Way Forward

Marilyn DeMars

iUniverse, Inc.
New York   Bloomington

The Way Forward

Copyright © 2008 by Marilyn M. DeMars

All rights reserved. No part of this book may be used or reproduced by any means, graphic, electronic, or mechanical, including photocopying, recording, taping or by any information storage retrieval system without the written permission of the publisher except in the case of brief quotations embodied in critical articles and reviews.

iUniverse books may be ordered through booksellers or by contacting:

iUniverse
1663 Liberty Drive
Bloomington, IN 47403
www.iuniverse.com
1-800-Authors (1-800-288-4677)

Because of the dynamic nature of the Internet, any Web addresses or links contained in this book may have changed since publication and may no longer be valid. The views expressed in this work are solely those of the author and do not necessarily reflect the views of the publisher, and the publisher hereby disclaims any responsibility for them.

ISBN: 978-0-595-53371-8 (pbk)
ISBN: 978-0-595-63428-6 (ebk)

Printed in the United States of America

Also by Marilyn DeMars

Sidetrack
The Way Back
I've Got This Brother
The Mistake

Chapter 1

As Jody Mitchell worked on a business ledger in the office of the Pinewood Motel, she was distracted by a child's voice singing *You Are My Sunshine*. Though for the past twenty minutes she'd been unconsciously listening to a steady stream of songs coming from the back yard, the sunshine one kept returning as obviously the child's favorite. Now hearing it for the umpteenth time, Jody's curiosity got the best of her and she had to go take a look.

She left her place behind the counter and went into the back room, a combination break room and storage room. Through the screen door she saw a little girl singing her heart out while swooshing about on the tire swing that hung from the oak tree. Jody stood just to the side of the door, out of sight so as not to interfere. It was unusual, a child playing out there. Singing no less. Not many guests who stopped at this remote up-north-in-the-woods motel had kids along, and of those who did none who found much appeal in an old swing.

She was a darling girl—likely six or seven, dark hair blowing about a cute face, blue shorts, pink tee shirt, sandals, and a quite good voice. She was a delight to watch and listen to. But when she eventually dropped the sunshine song for a different one again, Jody returned to the front office. Smiling to herself, she felt a nice lift and the goodness of this day. In addition to the pleasantry of the singing girl she felt a renewal of gratitude for the new life she'd made for herself this past year. She'd taken a big step, selling her old family home in Winona, Minnesota and moving up here to the northeastern tip of the state near the diminutive town of Myre.

Last fall she and her brother Don and their friend Elliot Treggor purchased the Pinewood Motel together. It was to be a new start for the three of them, something each of them desperately needed. Over the winter and spring months they'd done an extensive renovation to the place, carefully preserving its original rustic charm. Though the motel was virtually situated in a heavily wooded area, it was nevertheless on a main through road and drew enough business to be profitable.

Jody was still amazed that, for being only twenty-three, she co-owned a business. Her older brother Don, who had resided in the Myre area prior to his return to Winona a year ago, was now glad to be back. And Elliot, previous owner of his failed Treggor Motel in Winona, was ecstatic about taking on the Pinewood.

"I'm back," Elliot needlessly announced, bursting through the front door on his return from some afternoon errands.

Jody put a finger to her lips. "Listen."

He became aware of the child's singing. "Cute. So who's the—"

"A little girl...out back...swinging and singing."

Elliot started for the back door to have a look and Jody followed him. "Cute," he said again. "Sweet voice. Who does she belong to?"

"I'm assuming one of our guests."

Elliot shook his head. "We have no kids staying here. Truck driver in three and newly weds in five, that's it. No kids. Unless there was a new registry while I was gone."

Jody was puzzled. "No. But...uh...are you sure? I mean, with there not being any houses around here she couldn't just happen out of nowhere, could she?"

"Let's go talk to her," Elliot suggested.

They went outside, and as they approached the girl she stopped singing and swinging. Looped through the rubber tire, she looked at them as if expecting a reprimand. "I was just swinging here," she explained.

"Hey, no problem," Elliot assured her. "I'm Elliot and this is Jody. We're the owners of this place. We just want to know where you're from, being there are no houses close by."

She didn't answer, as if maybe she was thinking that she ought not to share such information with strangers.

"It's okay," Jody said softly, "you can trust us. What's your name?"

The girl's dark eyes were wary.

Elliot shrugged and said to Jody, "Maybe she doesn't have one."

The girl's silent mouth curved up a smidgen at the edges.

"How old are you?" he tried. "Sixteen?"

A giggle spilled out of her. "Seven."

"Name?" he proceeded.

"Mad."

Elliot squinted at her. "You don't look mad."

"It's my name. And I live down that road out front."

Jody glanced about the yard. There was no one else there besides the three of them. "Who are you with?"

"Nobody."

"But you have to be with someone."

The mystery child left the swing and started away. "I have to go now."

"Wait," Elliot said, "you can't just—"

She broke into a run.

"Something's definitely not right here," Jody asserted, as she and Elliot hurried after her.

Hey!" Elliot shouted as the little girl named Mad passed the backside of the motel and disappeared around the corner toward the front. "Wait! Where you going? *Jeez*, she's fast."

By the time he and Jody reached the front parking lot, Mad was already some distance down the dirt shoulder of the highway, running for all her worth.

Jody was going to keep going, but Elliot grabbed her arm, suggesting, "Let her go."

"We can't just let her go!"

"She must belong to someone somewhere."

"*Someone somewhere?*" Jody resented Elliot's easy surrender.

"I hope so," he said.

The girl disappeared around the turn in the road, and Elliot shifted his attention to the front of the Pinewood Motel. Every day he gave it at least one long, proud look, as he was doing now. Though he hadn't been able to keep his motel afloat in Winona, which he'd inherited from his father, this one held much more promise. Thirty-seven, slightly stocky, slightly graying hair, Elliot was an honest and caring person, a good guy who'd had enough hard knocks in his past to now deserve the payback of a better life. He believed this was it.

Jody, in jeans and a sweatshirt and looking more like a teenager than a motel proprietor, stood beside him in equal awe of their Pinewood. "Nice, huh?"

Elliot nodded. "I especially liked your idea of painting it barn red, over its previous gray. It presents itself well amidst its rustic surrounding."

"I told you it'd be perfect."

"Yeah, you did," he laughed. "Don and I disagreed with you at first, but you always kick up a fuss until you get your way."

She punched him in the arm. "Because I'm always right."

He clutched his arm in mock pain. "Hitting people is not right, nor nice, nor ladylike." He gestured at her outfit. "But then who's a lady, right?"

The Way Forward

She attempted to sock him again, but he ducked out the way.

Jody loved the Pinewood as much as Elliot did, and they stood together staring at it like a couple of proud parents.

"I hate to spoil this Kodak moment," Elliot eventually said, "but have you gotten any word from Don yet?"

"No," she had to say.

"It's been three days now, right?"

"That's right," she scowled at the imposing downer. "And the last time he took off without a word he was gone for eight years."

"Until you and I hunted him down and hauled his ass back to Winona last summer."

Jody moaned. "Why can't he ever just settle down? Why can't he—"

Elliot put his arm around her. "Come on, he hasn't disappeared this time. He's just away for some reason that we don't yet know. Don't jump to conclusions. He'll be back. Probably. I mean, he loves this motel as much as we do."

Jody drew a deep breath, trying to get past the drag Don's welfare was on her. Turning to gaze at the highway, she faced her newer concern. "I'm worried about her."

Elliot studied the road as well.

"We should've followed her to see where she went," Jody said.

"Yeah...maybe...I don't know. Too late now."

"You shouldn't have stopped me."

"Sorry."

Jody felt an all-to-familiar ache. At sixteen she'd given birth to an illegitimate baby girl, which she'd been forced by her then-living father to immediately give up. Now as another sweet child came into and out of her life so swiftly, it touched a nerve that seemed destined never to heal.

"Maybe she'll be back," Elliot offered about Mad.

As they headed toward the office together, the truck driver from number three came walking toward them, toting his travel bag.

"See you guys later," he said, depositing his key in Elliot's hand.

"Yeah, later, thanks," Elliot said. "Keep it on all eighteen."

The trucker, a regular Pinewood guest amidst his routine runs, went for his semi parked along the far edge of the parking lot. As he pulled out onto the highway he sounded his ultra loud horn several times and caught Elliot and Jody's good-bye waves.

"I proofed the latest ledger pages," Jody established, as they entered the office.

"Good." Elliot poured himself a mug of coffee from the pot on the counter. "You've become very good at this motel stuff, y'know?"

"I worked for you at the Treggor for over two years, didn't I? What do you expect?"

"Taught you everything I know, didn't I?" he gloated.

"And then beyond that I learned the other ninety percent of my job on my own, didn't I?"

"Don't get smart," he warned her.

Jody swung and Elliot ducked.

Benjamin Simon, their night-shift employee, arrived. "You two at it again?"

"Jody's always at it, you know that," Elliot said, generating another playful punch from her that connected this time. "Ouch!"

"*Lawdy, Miss Clawdy…*" Benjamin exclaimed, "I never know what I'm gonna walk in on around here."

He was a dependable employee, a widower in his mid fifties who routinely began work at four in the afternoon and stayed until eight in the morning. Bless him. They were long shifts, but with the office door locked and a buzzer outside for late arrivals, he managed to doze on the cot in the back room between watching TV and reading. The schedule seemed to suit him well.

It was only three fifteen. Benjamin had arrived earlier than usual today, having some special gardening projects around the grounds that he wanted to get done before being left alone to mind the office. Elliot went out to assist him, and Jody busied herself with some light cleaning in the office and back room.

When four o'clock came and Benjamin's outside work was finished, Elliot and Jody told him goodnight and left. Elliot had invited Jody to have supper with him at his place, and it was as natural for her to accept as it was for him to ask.

Together they walked the dirt path that led off from the back yard of the motel and wove through a thickness of trees to a cottage. It was a cute and cozy little place that had been included in the motel package. It was determined up front that it would be Elliot's home, since Don still owned a cabin just outside of Myre which Jody would share with him.

"What are we having?" she asked Elliot along the way.

"Food," he replied.

And she was okay with that.

Elliot fussed in the kitchen, while Jody lounged in an easy chair in the living room. Slouched as far down as she could go, with her legs draped over an arm of the chair, she was perfectly used to making herself at home there. And for as used to being there as she was, she knew she needn't offer a hand with the meal preparation because Elliot always insisted on doing it alone. After all, he'd been a self-sufficient bachelor for a good number of years following his divorce.

From where Jody sat she could watch the amusing little production he always made of his cooking. He danced from cupboard to cupboard, humming to himself, tossing food into pots and bowls, twirling a spatula in the air, enjoying himself. It never ceased to amaze her how amidst his crazy antics he could produce such fine meals.

When Elliot glanced up from his counter work and caught her grinning at him, he demanded, "*What*?"

"I like where we're at," she said, "that's all."

He laughed, wiped his hands on a towel and came into the living room to stand before her. "Where we're at?" he questioned.

"You…me…our motel…and—"

"Our relationship?" he asked, arching an eyebrow.

"Yeah, sure, I guess," Jody said.

"You guess?"

"It's comfortable, right? Our relationship?"

"For *you*, maybe," he teased. "For me it's constant lunacy."

"Thanks," she snarled playfully, although she could emphatically agree that the word lunacy often did fit the truth of them. They'd been through a lot of crazies together. One of them being that after three years of knowing each other, it was still questionable as to whether they were an actual couple or just friends. The ongoing acceptance the both of them had, to whatever way they were or weren't, was what made it a lunacy. But for the most part it was a *comfortable* sort of lunacy.

Jody popped out of her chair. "When do we eat? I'm starving."

"For sure you could use a little more meat on those bones of yours," he razzed her.

"And you could use a little less," she said, following him to the kitchen.

"I'd say we balance each other out," he laughed.

When she lifted the cover off the pot on the stove to take a peek, Elliot was right there putting it back, saying, "It'll be a while yet. Want a beer in the meantime?"

"Sure."

They sat at the kitchen table and chatted while supper cooked.

After Elliot's specialty chili and some French bread, Jody walked the path back to the motel by herself, stuck her head in the office to say goodnight to Benjamin, then drove the seven-mile distance to the cabin. Though the summer days were long, darkness seemed to have fallen amazingly fast tonight. Probably because she'd stayed at Elliot's much later than she'd intended.

Like Elliot's place, Don's cabin also sat in a clearing of trees, with that little-house-in-the-woods look. Jody entered, already feeling the emptiness of her brother's absence. He hadn't been there for days. He wasn't there now.

6

She couldn't help worrying that maybe he'd never be there again. Just when she'd finally come around to believing that he was living a more stable life now, he had to go and pull another disappearing act.

The cabin was one room, with dark walls and a bare wood floor. A fireplace and a few pieces of living-room furniture occupied one side, a kitchen area the other side, and a small bathroom in back. A loft bedroom stuck out over a section of downstairs.

Jody threw down her purse, kicked off her shoes, and climbed the ladder to the loft. When they'd taken up sharing Don's cabin, he'd given up his bed to her and took the couch for himself. He was a good brother…when he was around. Though Elliot had said they really shouldn't refer to Don's being gone as a disappearance, as far as she was concerned there was no other word for it.

Without changing into her nightclothes, Jody dropped onto the bed in an emotional frenzy. As if being stressed over her brother wasn't enough, she was also feeling a strong concern for that little singing-girl named Mad. Her own baby girl, somewhere out there in the unbeknownst, would now be Mad's age, and she couldn't help comparing the two of them. It was a good-bad feeling. Unsettling, like something demanding an answer of which she didn't even know the question.

It had helped, spending the evening with Elliot. He was good for her. She could always count on him to be witty and caring and charming and straightforward and uplifting. Except right now, all alone, nothing kept Jody from wishing that Don was home. And that her baby girl was with her. And that she didn't keep hearing Mad's sweet voice in her head, singing *You Are My Sunshine.* And that Elliot would've asked her to spend the night at his place. Except that he wasn't that kind of guy. Bold as he could be, he nevertheless was proper. She supposed she wasn't that kind of girl, either. Although… hadn't she been that kind eight years ago? With Kevin?

Lying there staring into the encompassing darkness and silence, Jody knew this was going to be an exceptionally long night.

Chapter 2

The sun had barely risen when Elliot left his cottage and strolled down the path to the motel. But he hadn't slept well and finally decided to get up and get going rather than lie in bed tossing and turning any longer. Jody had been on his mind throughout the night. So had her wayward brother. They were some pair, those two, both chaotically inclined. And caring about the both of them as he did usually drove Elliot into a chaotic state of his own.

Though he really hadn't thought Don would pull another disappearing act on his sister, the guy's four-day absence without so much as a word was surely making it look that way. It was driving Jody crazy. She was seeing this to mean that he'd dropped out of her life for another eight years, just like the last time he'd taken off. Elliot tried to keep her from thinking that, but day by day it was becoming harder for him.

Somewhere along the way it'd become his job to be Jody's rock. She seemed to need a lot from him, and he did his best to steady her world. But sometimes he didn't feel so steady himself. Times when this girl would turn to him with her needs and it would, in turn, make him keenly aware of his own needs. Times when maybe he should've talked to her about his wanting to be so much more to her than just her rock. But he always lost his nerve. *Oh, but what a wimp hides behind the rock,* he thought of himself.

"'Mornin'," Benjamin Simon greeted Elliot's entrance into the motel office. Standing behind the counter, he looked as bright-eyed and fresh as if he'd had at least nine hours of sleep. Maybe he had.

"Hey…" Elliot moaned amidst a yawn.

Benjamin checked the time. "You're not due for two hours. What's up?"

"Rough night. Couldn't sleep. You look well rested."

"No customers. Most all I do 'round here is eat, read, watch TV and sleep."

"You do it well. You're a good employee, Benjamin."

He shrugged modesty. "I try."

Elliot laughed. "Anyway, you can go ahead and take off now that I'm here."

Benjamin was hesitant to the offer until Elliot added, "With pay."

Then he nodded, raised his hands in praise, and headed for the door. "Thanks. See ya tomorrow."

Elliot poured himself a mug of coffee from the pot on the counter and hastily drank some like a drug fix. Then carrying it with him, he walked around the office. Feeling as lousy as he did was a pathetic way to start the day, and he needed to shake it.

Life was good, except for problems. Problems he couldn't fix turned into anxiety. Anxiety became draining. And lying awake wrestling with it most of the night proved to be of no help. This up-north life was supposed to be a new beginning. An escape from problems. Yet, in actuality, if there were no problems wouldn't he be dead? *Stop.* These thoughts were getting way too analytical on top of only a few hours of sleep.

All Elliot knew was that the trials and tribulations of Jody and Don were never long at rest. Plus there was something very unsettling about that little Mad girl that he couldn't let go of. And the whole Myre area was in a drought, to which he worried when and if they'd ever get the much-needed rain. And what about the occasional new aches that hammered his knees? Did that mean he was getting old? Or that he was carrying around fifteen pounds too many for his height? Thus should he attempt the diet and exercise route, or merely grow three inches taller?

Though walking helped lighten his spirit, he'd soon had enough exercise. He got a second cup of coffee and went to stand at the front window. Additionally uplifting was how the sun had now risen enough to come slanting gloriously through the trees across the road. It seemed to signify the promise of a good day. Despite the need for rain, the sun could lift the lowest of doldrums.

Much to his surprise, Jody soon came driving into the parking lot. She was never this early to her shift. Elliot was almost afraid to think what it might mean. When she got out of her car, slammed the door hard, and marched toward the office in an obvious huff, he crossed himself and rolled his eyes upward.

He opened the office door and she stormed on in past him, tossing her hands and sputtering, "He's not home yet!"

Elliot poured her some coffee and handed it to her. "Good morning."

"Couldn't sleep."

"Me neither."

After a few sips of the hot brew, Jody moaned, "What are we going to do?"

"*We?*" He faked his surprise, well knowing he was always automatically invited into her dilemmas.

Despite Jody's upset, her appearance was perky and fresh. Tan jeans, white shirt, dark hair tied in a ponytail with a yellow ribbon. Invariably nice to look at.

While Elliot was looking, she finished her coffee.

After a pause she squawked, "He can't do this again! I have to—"

"You can't keep trying to control Don."

"This isn't about control."

Elliot chuckled and shook his finger at her. "I think I know you better than you know yourself on this one."

Jody put her coffee mug on the counter and stuck her hands on her hips. "I just want him to settle down and stay put somewhere. It was his idea, this motel venture."

"It was," Elliot agreed.

She quoted Don's original words, "*The three of us, we'll move up north, go partners on the Pinewood, build new lives for ourselves.* Okay…so like now where is he?"

Elliot didn't have an answer.

"So…" Jody continued, "I don't know whether to be angry or worried."

"How about neither," Elliot advised her. "How about you just hang in there for a time yet? I think it's still too soon to feel either way."

Jody started to settle down. Good. She drew a deep breath and released it slowly. "Okay, I guess I can hang in there for a while yet. I'll try. Today I'll try not to dwell on my brother. Thanks, Elliot," she ended on a smile.

He shrugged. "No problem."

They met in the center of the office to exchange an affectionate hug. Problem solved for now, just like that. *Her* problem, not his. His problem of the moment was wondering how many more fond embraces it might take between them before they advanced to intimacy. *Real* intimacy. Or would they ever? And did it matter? The wonderment of their relationship both intrigued him and scared him. While trying to keep a non-committal attitude was surely the safest solution, is wasn't the easiest

"You look a little strange," Jody commented, stepping back from him.

"What can I say, I'm a strange guy."

"Yes, you are," she laughed, "and that's what I like best about you."

Elliot supposed it was an admirable quality. Thus he complimented her with the same, "Takes a strange one to know a strange one."

She punched him in the chest.

* * *

Later that morning the sweet singing voice of the little girl named Mad started up again in the back yard. Jody dropped what she was doing and hurried to the back door. "She's not going to run off from us today," she said as Elliot joined her.

He motioned to his sneakers. "Got my running shoes on."

The instant the two adults burst outside and toward her, the girl stopped singing and planted her feet against the ground to stop the swing.

"Okay," Jody began, gently but earnestly, "let's get things straight here."

"I…I didn't do anything wrong," the child said apologetically. "Did I?"

"No, no," Elliot assured her. "As we told you yesterday, we just want to know where you're from and something about you."

Switching her look from Elliot to Jody then back to Elliot again, she said, "I told you yesterday my name is Mad and I live down the road."

"Why did you take off from us like that?" Jody asked.

Mad left the swing and started to leave.

Elliot caught her by the arm. "No, you don't."

The child looked scared.

Jody motioned for Elliot to let go of her. "It's okay, Maddy, we—"

"It's Mad! I told you it's Mad!"

"I'm sorry. Yes, you did. Look, we don't mean to frighten you. We enjoy having you here. And your songs are a delight. We just want to make sure things are all right with you. As responsible adults, it's our job to do that."

The girl stayed put. And looking between the two of them again, she repeated, "I live down the road."

Elliot shook his head in puzzlement. "But there are no houses within—"

"You have to go off the road a ways, past a lot of trees. It's kinda hard to see."

"You live there with your parents," Jody assumed.

"My grandma."

"So where are your parents?" Elliot asked.

"I don't have a dad and I don't know where my mom is."

A wave of nausea hit Jody. She gave Elliot a *what-do-we-do-now*? look.

"I think we should meet your Grandma," he told Mad. "Why don't we drive you home and—"

"I don't go in cars with strangers," she stated.

Elliot and Jody exchanged glances, respecting as much.

The Way Forward

"We'll walk you home, how's that?" Jody suggested. "To meet your grandma."

Mad's dark eyes seemed to grow darker. She wasn't liking this nor cooperating any too readily. "My grandma isn't up yet."

"Then we'll wait outside the house till she does wake up," Elliot said. "It'll be okay, Mad. I think she'll be glad to meet us."

"Why do you want to meet her?" Mad asked.

"Because—" Jody started.

"—we're friendly people," Elliot finished.

A slight smile escaped Mad, and thus she began to walk, *not run*, allowing Elliot and Jody to join her.

On the way, Elliot locked both the back and the front motel office doors. Then the three of them cut across the front lot and started down the side of the highway. Mad was quiet, no song to her walking as there'd been to her swinging. She made frequent glances up at Jody and Elliot, as if trying to figure them out.

When the walk began to stretch beyond a seemingly half mile, Jody noticed Elliot's breathing shorten and her own legs tiring. Mad's seven-year old stamina, however, was holding up fine.

"So what's your real name?" Jody asked her.

"Mad."

"Come on," Elliot laughed, "that's a nickname to something else, right? Such as Madison?"

The girl didn't answer.

Elliot continued assuming, "So the common nickname for Madison would be Maddy, wouldn't it and not—"

The girl stopped walking. "Don't call me that!"

"Sorry."

"*Ever!*" the girl added.

"For sure," Elliot complied.

Mad started walking again, putting distance between them and leaving Jody and Elliot exchanging bewildered looks.

When they finally arrived at the place Mad called home, they indeed found it next to hidden. It stood at the end of a long private road off the highway, both sides thickly edged with trees.

"Wait here," Mad instructed Jody and Elliot, leaving them in the yard while she scurried forth to the rickety old house.

Before she even got to the porch steps, the front door sprung open and the supposed grandmother came bristling out in an unfriendly fashion.

"What's this?" she snarled, as though she never had visitors and didn't want any now. Wearing a bathrobe and looking only half-awake, the sixtyish woman squinted into the bright daylight.

"Jody and Elliot," Mad introduced them.

"We own the Pinewood Motel down the road," Jody explained. "Mad's been coming there on her own to swing on the tire swing in our back yard."

The grandmother rocked her head in a ho-hum way. "Yeah, I know. So that's a crime?"

"You knew about it?" Elliot verified. "That she came down there alone?"

The woman shrugged. "I don't know all the places she goes. She goes a lot."

"And that doesn't worry you?" Jody asked.

"She's a responsible child."

"She's *seven*," Elliot said.

The grandmother came down the steps and into the yard to more closely examine the motel people. Whereas Jody and Elliot had come to investigate her, it suddenly seemed like they were the ones under scrutiny. "What the hell are you two up to anyway? What do you want here?" she questioned them.

Elliot motioned behind him toward the road. "It's a long walk down that highway to our motel. It could be risky for Mad, going it alone."

"Like that's your business?" the woman scoffed.

"We've made it be, yes," Jody said.

The grandmother held a hand over her heart. "Look…I'm doin' my best here. With the girl. Far better'n her ma ever did, that's for sure. I trust Mad. I have to. Can't keep her locked up, can I? Ain't much for her to do 'round here. I want her to be happy. God knows I want her to be happy. That's all there is to it. My name's Claire. Nice to meet you, Jody and Elliot, but please now go back to your hotel and don't concern yourself with us."

"Motel," Elliot corrected her.

"We don't mind Mad playing there," Jody continued nevertheless, "it's just that we're bothered as to how she gets there."

"Don't be," Claire said.

"I never got hit by a car," Mad spoke up, as if to save her grandmother as well as herself.

Elliot tested her. "And what if some car stopped and a man jumped out of it to talk to you and—"

"I'd run away from him real fast," Mad answered before hearing the whole scenario.

"Yeah, well you can sure run, we know that," he said with a chuckle.

Claire threw up her hands, turned and started back inside. "Case closed. I've got things to do. Come on, Mad, you've got chores."

"Wait!" Jody said, daring to follow Mad onto the porch. She handed her a business card. "Both our motel and home phone numbers are on it. If you

The Way Forward

ever need us, or want to call us about anything at all, or nothing at all, please do. Hang onto it, okay?"

The girl nodded, stuck the card into her pocket, and went inside the house.

Jody and Elliot began their walk back to the motel.

"I'm not exactly satisfied with that little meeting," Jody concluded.

"I know what you mean," Elliot said.

The walk back to the Pinewood actually seemed longer than the walk from it. About halfway into the distance Elliot let out a moan.

"You okay?" Jody asked him.

He paused to catch his breath. "You walk too fast. We didn't walk this fast with Mad."

"Sorry." She started walking at a slower pace, and he was more comfortable with that. "I'm really worried about her," Jody said.

"Me too. Like how can she walk this far and not have a heart attack?"

Jody laughed. "She's seven. And you're not going to have a heart attack, Elliot. You just obviously need to get out and do this more often. You and me…we should go for walks more often."

"Right. Shorter ones."

"It's kind of amazing, isn't it?" Jody said dreamily.

"Our walking?"

She shook her head at his silliness. "That my baby…she's also seven now."

"I know," Elliot said.

Jody felt glad that he knew.

Chapter 3

Getting back to the business of the motel, Elliot checked in two new guests and Jody cleaned the room the truck driver left yesterday. She didn't mind cleaning rooms. She found it rather gratifying. Fresh linens, fluffed pillows, fragrant cleaning solutions, dusting, vacuuming, straightening up. A nicely readied room was the pride of a good motel. And sometimes the decisive generosity of a guest. The truck driver always left a $10 tip on the nightstand for her. Jody smiled and tucked the money into her pocket.

"She's so cute," she commended to Elliot on her return to the office.

He looked up from the counter. "Huh? Oh…the swinger-singer? Yeah."

Mad was continually on Jody's mind, a mixture of wonderment and worry and delight. "Why do you suppose she hates being called Maddy?"

Elliot laughed. "Living with that strange grandmother of hers, maybe the name Mad helps her stay tough enough to cope."

"What's your impression of Claire?"

"Like I just said, strange. Not a great role model for bringing up a little girl."

"I wonder about Mad's mother and if she—"

"Maybe we shouldn't wonder so much about Mad and her family," Elliot suggested.

"Impossible."

"I know."

Jody flaunted her tip money at him.

"I get half," he said.

"You clean half the room, you get half the tip."

"Y'know," he whined, "it's not fair that I do all the hard stuff around here and you get the perks."

The Way Forward

Jody glanced over the counter edge, noting the crossword puzzle he was currently involved with. "Right."

"I'm on my break," he claimed.

"Somebody's got to look out for her." Jody's concern was already back on Mad. "She's obviously not in good hands with that grandmother of hers."

Elliot closed his crossword book and slid it aside. "From what we've seen, no."

"We need to step in and do something."

Elliot moaned. "Here it comes."

"I'm going out back to think." Jody cut through the break room and went outside to the tire swing. She sat in it, hoping to acquire a closer connection to Mad's being. She wondered if the girl would come back again today, or ever, after they'd strongly enforced that she not walk the road by herself again. Jody felt a sad sense of already missing her.

Elliot soon came outside, finding Jody on the swing and giving her a push so hard it took her breath away. She screamed and he pushed her again. She giggled and he pushed her still harder. When she'd had enough, she begged him to stop.

He caught the rope and brought her to a stop, laughing, "What'sa matter, too old for this stuff?"

"*You* get in," she challenged him, "and let me push *you* like that."

"No thanks, I just finished eating a snack."

"You're supposed to be helping me think of something to do about Mad, you know."

"Eating helps me think."

"So what have you come up with?"

"Nothing. It was an insufficient snack."

That afternoon, when Jody and Elliot were again in the back yard, this time pulling weeds in one of the flower gardens, the desk bell sounded out to them from the front office. *A customer.*

Elliot eagerly hurried inside, with Jody right behind him. When he stopped short she ran smack into him.

The bell-ringer was Don.

"Where the hell have you been?" Elliot blasted Jody's brother.

Holding a blond-haired young woman under his arm, Don's handsome face exploded into a big devilish grin.

Jody marched toward him with her hands on her hips. "You did it again, didn't you! You think you can just take off whenever without any explanation or—"

"Whoa!" Don spoke above her. "My intention was to surprise you guys. I'd like you to meet Nora. She and I just returned from our honeymoon. We were married in Vegas."

The couple held forth their left hands, displaying matching wedding bands.

Then the bride offered her right hand to Jody, saying, "Nice to meet you Jody. I've heard a lot about you."

Jody hesitated shaking with her sister-in-law. *Sister-in-law?* This was just too weird. And if she actually touched this person it might make it real, which would be even more weird. But Nora was waiting and Jody felt forced. When they shook, Jody was surprised at the notable warmth in Nora's gesture.

As Nora went on to shake hands with Elliot, Don gave Jody a brotherly hug.

Hugs worked wonders on Jody and she could only say, "I'm glad you're all right."

"I'm more than all right, little sister," he said, bursting with excitement. "But I'm sorry to have worried you. I guess I was selfishly off in my own little world."

"*Our* little world," his wife clarified.

Don turned to give Nora a kiss.

"Well, well…" Elliot said, as if he were trying as hard as Jody to rise above his own qualms, "so how did all of this come about, if I may be so bold as to ask."

"Nora tends bar at Maxy's in Myre and—"

"You're supposed to be staying *out* of bars, remember!" Jody scowled, in reference to his past drinking problem.

Don held up a promise hand. "I hadn't been in there for ages. I only stopped in a couple weeks ago on a harmless whim, and that's when I met Nora. And then I started visiting Maxy's on a frequent basis, needless to say."

"He hasn't been drinking, if that's what you're concerned about," Nora offered.

Jody gave the wife a hard look. Nora certainly didn't know her well enough to have any idea of the extent of concern she might or might not have. And if she thought she knew Don well enough to marry him after only a couple weeks, she was crazy.

Elliot slid an arm around Jody, as a warning for her to be careful. Though he himself couldn't keep from sardonically verifying, " Only *two weeks* you guys have known each other?"

Don and Nora nodded in sync then shared another kiss.

Oh, how Jody wished her big brother would grow up. This was just so ultimately stupid of him. A mistake that could not easily be undone. Okay, she supposed what was done was done for the moment. But aside from all that was going on, there was a motel to run. Speaking intentionally cool to him, she asked, "So I guess now that you're back you could do a shift and give Elliot and me a break?"

The Way Forward

Don gave her a *you've-got-to-be-kidding* smirk. Then he took Nora's hand and started leading her out of the office. "I'll make up my time starting tomorrow. Promise. See you at home later, Jody."

"Home…" she repeated under her breath as the office door closed behind Mr. and Mrs. Mitchell.

Elliot scratched his head and chuckled. "Well, whatd'ya think of that?"

"I think I'm more worried about my brother now that he's back than when he was missing."

Elliot watched Don's car pull out of the front lot. "Yeah, me too."

* * *

"This is it," Don said, carrying Nora over the threshold of his cabin. Because things had happened so fast for them, the reality of his actually having a wife now was still a little on the blurry side. Thus he kind of felt more like he was toting home an awarded sports trophy rather than a wife… FASTEST LOVER IN THE WORLD. He kissed her for verification of her realness. She was much more than a trophy.

When he put her back down onto her feet, she took a deep breath and gazed about, finding that she could see everything there was to see from that one spot.

The shock of it was over quickly however, and her face crinkled into a smile. "It's nice. It's cozy. It's—"

"—cheap," Don said.

They laughed, then drew together into another long, passionate kiss. The honeymoon was definitely still on, following their wedding of three days ago.

"I can't believe you haven't brought me here before now," Nora said.

"I can't believe a lot of things about us," he responded.

"Two weeks…" she seductively actualized the length of their relationship. "You certainly swept me off my feet, Don Mitchell."

He smiled proudly and motioned to the loft ladder. "The bedroom's up there."

She twisted out of his embrace with a giggle. "Would you mind if I bring my things in and unpack first?"

"Oh…yeah…sure…our bags."

Don was so in love he could hardly stand it. He thought he'd felt the height of love with a girl named Krista, back in Winona years ago. But he'd been no more than a kid then, and what had he really known? Not enough to know that she'd never really appreciated him. Heck, he hadn't even appreciated himself back then.

After Krista broke up with him he'd left home and disappeared into a world away from everyone, including his kid sister Jody and his father. He hadn't even been aware of his father's dying until a year ago, when Jody and Elliot managed to locate him.

Don had been madder than hell when they'd literally forced him back to Winona, insisting that a reconnection there was what he needed. But eventually he found its rewards. He helped Jody fix up their old family home and sell it. He made a formal closure with Krista, who by then was married and pregnant. He located the Pinewood Motel and talked Elliot and Jody into going together on it with him. And now, after some tough life lessons, he was back in Myre, where just two weeks ago he'd discovered the town's whole new allure, Nora.

Time seemed to come to a standstill in the most lazy, hazy, wonderfully romantic sort of way. Spending the rest of the afternoon together in the loft bed, Don and Nora felt as if they were the only two people in the whole world, and total bliss was their wedding gift to each other.

Until the cabin door slammed downstairs.

Jody was home.

Don pulled on his jeans and went down the ladder. "Hey…" he greeted his sister, choking back his resentment of her intrusion.

"Hey," she responded coolly, hands on hips and eyes gazing upward.

Nora was looking down at her from the loft railing. "Hi, Jody."

Jody said nothing to her new sister-in-law. She marched over to the couch and plunked down in a huff. Don was all too familiar with this demeanor of hers and gave an internal huff of his own.

Jody again looked up at the loft. "My room."

Don nervously rocked from foot to foot before her. *Damn the guilt she made him feel.* "Yeah…well…uh, I know that it was. But now I've got Nora here and…I, uh… guess we'll have to make a switch, Jody. I mean, that's just the way it is."

Jody patted the cushion beside her, verifying, "My new room."

Nora was dressed and coming down the ladder, sensing the brother-sister tension. "My place was even smaller than this," she told Jody, as if she thought that would brighten the matter. "I had a room over the garage at the Wilson's. I let it go already, because Don said—"

"This is Don's place," Jody sharply offered justification. "If he wants to bring in a bride and take over my loft bedroom he can. No problem." She folded her arms across her chest.

Don supposed he was really in for it, with these two women in his small cabin. But he knew that when a guy marries, he must naturally put his wife first.

Putting an arm around Nora, he told his sister, "Don't get bent, okay?"

Jody gave him an uncompromising look.

"Heck," Don added, "we'll all be working our jobs most of the time."

"Except at night," Jody said. She left the couch and headed for the ladder. "I'll bring my stuff down. I don't have that much."

Obviously feeling now that *she* was the imposition, Nora apologized to Jody. "I'm sorry. I didn't know Don's place was this small."

"You don't know a lot of stuff about my brother," Jody exclaimed. "But I'm sure it will be a learning experience."

As Jody disappeared up the ladder, Don whispered to Nora, "It'll be all right, honey. We're all going to do just fine together, you'll see."

He glanced up at the loft, finding Jody ruefully looking down from it.

Chapter 4

"Good-morning," Jody mumbled to the newly weds as they came down the loft ladder into the kitchen the next morning.

Don mumbled something undetectable back to her as he poured himself a mug of coffee from the pot she'd brewed.

Nora was more pleasantly awake. "Good-morning, Jody. Mmm, coffee smells great. You sleep all right on the couch?"

Jody ignored her for Don. "Going to work today?"

"I suppose," he said amidst a yawn.

"You *suppose*? That sounds real promising."

Suddenly her brother and his bride were locked into a close embrace and a long kiss. Jody knew this was supposed to be a nice thing, Don in love and married, but it was hard for her to accept it so far.

Dressed in a pale-blue negligee meant only for one's spouse to view, Nora unashamedly helped herself to some coffee while telling Jody, "I'm going to be working day shifts now instead of night shifts at the bar. Except for Saturdays, that is. Unfortunately I'll still have to work Saturday nights, but I'll have Sundays and Mondays off."

Jody nodded, as if she cared.

And Nora continued, as if she had a listener. "Good compromise, wouldn't you say, since I have a husband to consider now?"

"Nice," Jody agreed with a bitter tongue.

Nora was notably discomforted by Jody's manner and tried to get past it. "Don and I will have plenty of time together."

"You mean, to get to know each other?"

"Newly married couples need time to do that, yes."

"Shouldn't that come *before* the marriage?"

The Way Forward

Jody received disturbed looks from the honeymooners. And then suddenly Don was whisking her outside as if she'd said or done something wrong.

"Is this the way it's going to be?" he snarled at her in the yard, letting her go with a shove that sent her stumbling backwards.

"I don't know...is it?" Jody said, not yet out of wisecracks.

"It sure as heck wouldn't hurt for you to be a little warmer to my wife."

She stuck her hands on her hips. "Excuse me if I'm a little slow warming up to that fact that my brother disappears, worrying Elliot and me to no ends, then comes back married to some stranger who happens to tend bar, despite his having a drinking problem. I'm sorry, but all this has left me pretty cold, yes."

Don shook his head and rolled his eyes. "You worry about all the wrong things, you know that, Jody? Okay, again...I'm sorry for worrying you and Elliot. But as for Nora, she's good for me and I think I'm good for her. I've never felt this happy, ever. It's a great feeling, don't spoil it for me. And just because Nora serves liquor doesn't mean I'm going to drink it. Gimme a damn break here, will you!"

Angry as Jody was, she almost lost it with an urge to crack a smile at Don's dramatic speech. But she stubbornly hung tough. "Why don't you give yourself a break and grow up."

He gave her a barbed grin. "*Me* grow up? That's cute. Nora and I know what we're doing. We both knew what we wanted and there was no reason to play the dating game for six months."

"Oh, right! You can always get to know each other later on."

"Right, *at least before having a kid*."

Jody took his low blow hard about herself and Kevin. She walked around Don and started for the cabin. "Gotta get my purse and go to work."

"Jody, I'm sorry..." Don said to her back. "I didn't mean to—"

She slammed the cabin door on his apology, which in a double effect startled Nora, causing her to drop a plate on the kitchen floor.

*   *   *

Elliot felt Jody's mood the instant she walked into the motel office. "Rough night, huh," he said to her slow shuffle, slumped shoulders, and pouty mouth.

She threw her purse at the deacon's bench below the front window, saying nothing.

"So is Don coming in today?" Elliot asked carefully, as if he were in harm's way.

"He supposes so," Jody said calmly, ahead of blowing up. "He's so screwed up, that brother of mine!"

Jeez, was she ever going to quit trying to own him? *Talk about being screwed up...* for a long time Elliot had wondered which of the brother-sister duo deserved that claim more.

"*What?*" she demanded of his staring.

He managed a smile, but was not about to confess his thought.

"Don't you think so?" Jody asked.

"Huh?" He'd lost the place of their conversation.

"That Don's so screwed up?"

"Well, uh...he just got married, y'know," Elliot tried bringing some common sense into it. "Marriage is not a crime, Jody. Let him alone. You've got your own life to live."

"What life?" she fired back at him. "Like I really have one."

"You have the motel. And me."

She dipped her head and looked at him from the tops of her eyes, as if he'd just told her a stupid joke.

"You're saying that me and the Pinewood mean nothing to you?" he interpreted. "Thanks," he laughed, as if the put down were nothing.

"I'm referring to where I am. Stuck in the woods with no social life whatsoever."

"Social life? You never needed one before. I thought you were happy about this arrangement, Jody."

"I was. I am. I'm...just feeling frustrated."

"Over Don?"

"Not just Don."

Elliot shrugged. "What then?"

She tossed her hands into the air. "Everything!"

"That's a lot of frustration."

"Yes."

"So how can I help you alleviate your frustration?"

"*You?*" she screeched. "You're part of it."

"Huh?" Elliot stood totally lost as she stormed off to the back room.

* * *

Jody was feeling much calmer when Don arrived an hour later. She behaved apologetically and sisterly-sweet toward him. "Sorry about earlier."

He smiled and returned the nicety. "Me, too. I got way out of line with what I shot off at you."

"Me, too."

The Way Forward

"C'mere…" he pulled her close for a hug.

"Nora's not so bad," she told him.

He laughed. "No, she's not bad at all."

"This has been a shock, Don. A really big shock." She backed away from him to give him a straight look.

"I know. A good shock though. Come on, you gotta see it that way."

She felt his persuasiveness. How could she not. She nodded, complying with, "You deserve to be happy."

"So do you."

She grinned playfully. "Maybe if I hung out at Maxy's I might meet the love of my life, too."

"You've got Elliot."

She closed her eyes, dreaming of more. "I'd like to feel what real love is. I thought it was Kevin. Boy, was I stupid and wrong. I…I'd just like to know real love. But how will I ever know it, recognize it if it does come along?"

"You will." Don laughed. "When cupid shoots you with an arrow, you'll know."

She scrinched her face. "Ouch."

He nodded. "It gets your serious attention, that's for sure."

"What does?" Elliot asked, coming into the office, curious of the conversation he'd just missed.

"*You* do," Don told him.

"Yep," he played along, "everywhere I go. So…you here to work?"

"I am."

"Good." Elliot motioned to a box of papers on the counter. "Jody and I have been getting rid of unnecessary stuff around here, and we've been waiting for you to give this stack your eagle eye before we trash it."

"Sure. I can do that."

"Also, now that you're here, Jody and I would like to take off for the rest of the day. We haven't had a real break all the while you've been gone."

"I think I can handle things till Benjamin comes in. Sure. But…"

"But what?" Jody sensed a whole new problem for the look on her brother's face.

"I've been thinking…I'd really like to go back to my old logging job."

It was a whole new problem all right. "This motel idea was yours, you know," she sharply reminded him.

"I know," he said, stuffing his hands into his pants pockets and lowering his gaze from hers. "But with all the renovation work done around here, I…I just don't think I'm cut out for baby sitting the office."

Jody was going to say something, but Elliot stopped her in order to make his own comment to Don. "If that's what you want, so be it. We'll manage."

It was a quick decision that Jody wasn't part of and wasn't sure she liked. So as a compromise, she tagged a condition onto it. "You'll have to find your own replacement then."

"Sure. I will," Don agreed. "So where are you two going on your well-deserved break?

"We don't know yet," Jody said, leaving with Elliot.

"I'll drive," he said. They got into his car, and before pulling onto the highway, he asked, "Which way?"

"Left."

Just a short distance down the highway, Jody cried out, "*Stop!*"

Elliot slammed on the brakes. "*Jeez! What?*"

She motioned to the other side of the road. "Mad...coming this way. We told her not to do this by herself. She doesn't listen. I've got to talk to her."

"I'm not sure if—"

"I'm sure," Jody said, already getting out of the car.

Elliot went across the road with her.

Mad was bright and cheery and unmindful that yesterday they'd scolded her about this very thing. She was happily surprised, meeting up with the motel people on her way.

Until Jody lit into her. "You can't do this! You were told not to do this anymore!"

"My grandma's okay with it," Mad fended.

"Your grandma—" Jody caught herself from saying anything sinister about the woman, "no, I don't think she is. She can't possibly be okay with it."

"This isn't a safe thing for a kid to be doing," Elliot reminded Mad.

The girl looked back and forth between the two of them, eyes beginning to shimmer. She was innocent and unimaginable of what was wrong with her life. Just as Jody's own little girl might be at this time, wherever she was.

"How would you like to spend the day with us?" Jody asked.

"Yeah, how about it?" Elliot also asked Mad.

The girl showed some interest, but was quiet and cautious.

Elliot reasoned, "If your grandma doesn't mind you walking all the way down to the motel alone, she wouldn't mind your going somewhere with us."

Mad shrugged her small shoulders as a maybe.

Jody further reasoned, "We're not strangers. We're Jody and Elliot, owners of the motel with the tire swing that you've been visiting."

Mad smiled. "Where would we be going?"

"We don't know yet," Elliot said, "but we'd love to have you come along."

The Way Forward

Mad giggled.

"Come get in the car," Jody said, taking her across the road by the hand. "We'll stop to let your grandma know. Okay?"

"Okay," Mad said.

When they got to the house, Jody got out of the car and approached the porch, where Claire was sitting in a rocker. She easily noticed a bottle of whiskey sitting on the floor beside her.

"Elliot and I would like to take Mad for a ride, if that's all right with you," Jody said with no beating around the bush.

The woman gave her a glazed look.

"Elliot and I own the Pinewood Motel," Jody reminded her. "Mad's been coming down there to swing on our tire swing. We met you yesterday, remember?"

"Oh…I guess…"

Jody motioned to the car behind her. "We have your granddaughter. We'd like to take her with us on a little outing."

Claire looked beyond Jody, catching a wave from Mad in the back seat of the car. Claire waved back at her. "I suppose it'd be okay."

"Really?" Jody squealed, having expected to have to fight for permission.

Claire gave no further words. She picked up her bottle and took a drink. It was obvious that the woman only wanted to be left alone again.

"So…." Elliot said, starting back to the highway as soon as Jody was back inside the car, "where would you girls like to go?"

Jody gave Mad a look over her shoulder. "You decide."

Mad's idea came quickly. "A picnic? Could we go on a picnic? My grandma never wants to go on one. She says they're silly."

"Exactly why they're so much fun," Elliot exclaimed. "We'll pick up some food in Myre and when lunch time rolls around we'll have found the perfect location to stop and eat."

That such place turned out being in the shade of some tall poplars near a babbling creek and scatters of wild flowers.

"I know it's your name," Jody said to the child, as they sat in the grass munching sandwiches and chips, "but couldn't we please call you something more cheerful? I mean, wouldn't you *like* being called something more cheerful?"

"My real name is Madison," she affirmed. "But my grandma started calling me Mad when she started taking care of me a year ago 'cause she said I always seemed mad."

"Were you? Are you? Mad?" Elliot asked.

"Sometimes. But not so much anymore. Mostly after my Mom left."

"Where'd she go?" Jody asked.

"I don't know. She just went."

Jody and Elliot exchanged sorrowful looks.

"Why won't you let us call you Maddy?" Jody asked, in spite of knowing how upset the girl became to it yesterday.

"No!" Mad loudly sounded her answer.

"Why?" Elliot pleaded. "What've you got against Maddy?"

"No!" Mad repeated even louder than before. "Don't call me that! Ever!"

"Okay, okay…" Jody said, sorry for having pushed where she shouldn't have.

The girl simmered and took another bite of her sandwich.

"Is your grandma good to you?" Jody asked.

Mad shrugged, as if she wasn't quite sure what good meant.

"In the general sense," Elliot added. "You know…good meals, clean clothing, cookies and hugs, a few hard rules?"

Mad shrugged. "She loves me."

Jody smiled, feeling somewhat assured that if the girl felt loved her home life couldn't be all that bad. But on the other hand Jody honestly wasn't sure if that made her feel better or worse. Like maybe *she* wanted to be the one who loved Mad. Maybe she already did.

It was hard saying good-bye when they dropped Mad back home. "Should I go in with you and make sure everything's all right in there?" Jody offered.

Mad paused beside Jody's window. "No, that's okay. Grandma usually sleeps all afternoon. I wake her up when I have supper ready."

"You do the cooking?" Elliot asked with a gulp.

Mad shrugged as if of course.

"You have our phone numbers if you need us," Jody reminded her.

Mad nodded. "Thanks for taking me on the picnic. It was fun. Bye."

Watching Mad run to the house and up the porch steps made Jody want to say something, but before she could Elliot gently advised her, "Don't."

He turned the car around, drove the inner road back to the highway, and headed for the motel.

"It was a fun time with Mad," Jody said.

"Yeah."

"So why am I feeling sad?"

"Probably the same reason I am."

Somehow his saying that made Jody feel a little better. Not a lot, but a little.

Chapter 5

Benjamin arrived for his night shift at the motel, Elliot and Don got into a discussion about a couple problem files, and Jody left for the cabin.

Nora was already there. Busily working in the kitchen, it appeared that she was making supper. *Jody's job.*

"I just got here fifteen minutes ago," Nora said. "I didn't know what you might be planning for supper, but I thought I'd just go ahead and start something."

"Oh," Jody responded.

"Hope that's okay."

"Sure."

"Hope you like cheesy chicken and rice."

Before Jody could answer, Nora added, "You can help if you'd like. You can make the salad."

Jody approached the kitchen counter, where a head of lettuce awaited.

"Don just loves chicken," Nora exclaimed as if she were telling Jody something she didn't already know.

Jody rolled her eyes and kept quiet. She tore lettuce leaves and placed them into a bowl, feeling like a guest in her own home. Now, suddenly, it was Nora's home.

When Don arrived, he and Nora greeted one another with kisses hot enough to make Jody turn away in embarrassment. And after they all sat down to eat, she became aware of them playing footsie beneath the table. Jody soon lost her appetite, as if she'd ever had much of a one to start with. Only halfway finished with her plate, she excused herself and went to sit on the couch with a book. No one seemed to pay much attention to what she was or wasn't doing. The newlyweds were too wrapped up in each other.

Jody made frequent glances at them over the top of her book. She didn't trust Nora. There was just something about that blond, curly hair of hers, the way it tumbled around her face and to her shoulders. And the way her nose crinkled when she laughed at the cutesy little things Don babbled to her. And the way she continually fussed over him with a continual compulsion to touch him. And the way Don sucked it all up so foolishly.

He helped Nora do dishes and clean up the kitchen, the two of them giggling and cooing as if the event were something romantically intimate. To Jody it was a distraction that caused her to reread the same page more than once.

When the lovebirds finished they turned out the kitchen light and climbed the ladder to the loft.

Jody thought *fine*, now she could finally concentrate on her book. But the sounds coming from upstairs were even more distracting.

Finally she closed her book with a thud, left the couch and went outside. An evening chill had set in. She hugged herself, wishing she'd grabbed her sweatshirt on the way out.

The quiet she found outside of the cabin was not entirely peaceful, for with it came a heavy sense of loneliness. Inside, Don and Nora had each other. While their actions sickened Jody, she couldn't deny feeling envious. And now, in addition to them, her mind once again spun with unsettling thoughts of the little girl named Mad…worry, confusion, frustration and delight.

Jody felt certain that there was a special reason for Mad's dropping into her life as she had. A reason for her to have already acquired a strong sense of responsibility toward the girl. Like maybe it was going to be up to her to report Mad's unstable home life to Child Welfare. Or maybe she would find it best to bypass Child Welfare and personally handle the situation on her own. For sure somebody had to do something, and for sure Jody felt like the chosen one to start the proper action. She and Elliot would talk about it tomorrow. They were good together on figuring things out.

Gazing upward at the sky, Jody spoke softly to God. "Thank you for Elliot."

* * *

"Am I right in noticing that your sister seemed to have left in somewhat of a huff?" Nora said to Don after the two of them were left alone in the cabin the next morning.

The Way Forward

Don grabbed his toast out of the toaster and joined her at the table. "You're going to find that Jody's little huffs are a regular part of who she is."

"I'm not sure she likes me," Nora determined.

Don stretched across the table to kiss her on the cheek. "Trust me… Jody's weird nature has nothing to do with you, only with whoever's around at the moment." He buttered his toast and reached for the jam.

"I mean, I like her and I'm sorry if I offend her in some way."

"You don't. Trust me. She's her own worst enemy." Taking a bite of toast, Don smiled at Nora with the wonderful amazement hitting him all over again that she was actually his wife. He'd never been happier in his life.

Only one thing was missing. His old logging job. Now that the remodeling work at the Pinewood was completed, he craved still more physical labor—that of working with trees and intricate equipment and his old buddies on the crew. Sitting around the motel just wasn't him.

"You've got an awfully deep look on your handsome face," Nora observed.

"Just thinking," he said.

"About?"

"Us."

"Mind sharing those thoughts about *us* with me?"

"Your work at the bar…" he began.

"Yeah?"

"You could do better than that, Nora."

"Excuse me?" She blinked her eyes with puzzlement.

"I want to go back to my logging job, and I've been thinking that maybe you could quit Maxy's and go to work at the motel as my replacement."

Nora was hauntingly silent for a few minutes. The calm before the storm. Then she upped from the table, scuffing her chair against the bare floor and bellowing in protest, "You've been thinking about what I should do with my life? Like now that you're my husband you think you're going to run it?"

Her Jody-like manner of behavior alarmed Don. "No. That's not it. Come on, Nora…it's a suggestion, only a suggestion. Like you could—"

"You know how much I like what I do."

"Yeah, sure, I know, but—"

"Is this why you wanted to marry me, thinking you'd have an easy replacement for your motel job so that you could go back to logging?"

"That's really stupid, Nora." Don grasped his head and moaned. He grimaced at how something so simple on his part could turn into something so treacherous on hers.

"I don't like controlling men."

"I'm not trying to control you," he said, aware that his voice was growing louder. "I'm just trying to talk to you about an idea."

"*Your* idea, not mine."

"Shit! Aren't I allowed to get one?"

"I'm not liking this side of you."

"Well, I'm sorry," Don said in a sarcastic drawl, "but I'm afraid you bought the whole package when you married me."

In one swift, continuous movement Nora grabbed her purse and stormed out of the cabin, slamming the door behind her. Her car roared out of the driveway.

Don remained at the table, feeling totally dumbfounded. Wondering if this was the first sign that maybe life beyond the honeymoon wasn't going to be quite as great as he'd thought. And, *please no*, but was Nora really going to turn out to be another Jody?

He poured himself more coffee. Gazing over at the cupboard that once stored his booze, he realized now, for the first time in a long time, how much he missed drinking at the onset of stress. He could sure use a drink right now. But he'd been dry for too long to give in to that demon again. He supposed he and Nora would talk more about this job stuff tonight. Maybe, until then, it might be wise of him to practice up on something good that he could say to her to help set the honeymoon back on track.

* * *

Jody could tell Elliot was reading her the moment she entered the motel office for the way he sat behind the counter, shaking his head and observing her with that *what-now?* look.

"It's awful!" she denounced. "With that woman in my place."

"Don's wife," he easily assumed.

"Yes."

"*Your* place?" he questioned.

"*Don's* place…his and that woman's now. I don't have one, a place. She's completely taken over. First my bedroom, then the cooking, then—"

"Don's wife," Elliot firmly reminded her.

Jody leaned an elbow on the counter and sighed. "If you can actually believe that."

Elliot laughed. "You mean you haven't asked to officially see their marriage certificate yet?"

"I don't like this," Jody stated.

"Do you have to? All you need to do is adapt."

"Why should I? I've been there longer than her."

The Way Forward

"Don's wife," Elliot stressed. Then grinning slyly, he concluded, "You're jealous."

Jody straightened up and planted her hands onto her hips. "That's sick."

"You're possessive of Don."

"I am not."

"Then what's this really all about, Jody? So your brother got married, so what? And the cabin got a little crowded, so what?"

"So *what?*" she fended. "Like I need to do something about it, that's what!"

Elliot laughed. "Like throw Nora out?"

She didn't appreciate his incessant sense of humor on this. Her eyes searched his for something more. He and she were always so together on things. Why not now when she so badly needed his support? Resorting to the fact that she probably needed to spell it out for him, she said, "I think it's best that I throw *myself* out."

Elliot went silent.

"Let me move in with you," she said.

More silence.

"You've got room," she continued. "More room than Don's place."

Elliot came alive, shaking his head and saying but one word. "No."

"Why?"

"You know why. It ain't right."

Jody narrowed her eyes at him. "How?"

"Don's your brother, I'm not."

"But you could be *like* my brother," she pleaded.

Elliot gave it a moment of thought but hardly a yes. "That kiss you and I shared…last fall…remember? It was not a brother-sister kiss. No, Jody, I don't think that you and I—"

"One kiss. Last fall. Whatever it may have been, it doesn't count. I need a place."

"You have a place. Small and uncomfortable, I'll grant you, but—"

"It's not going to work with me and her both there. I need out."

"You need to give this a chance, Jody."

"I have."

"Yeah, right," he said out the side of his mouth.

"You've gotta take me in."

Their conversation was suddenly interrupted by Mad's singing out back. That was all it took for Jody to forget the urgency of her sleeping place, and she hurried to the back door.

Elliot followed. "She's already been out there for a while. I told her to stop doing this, coming down the road alone. I told her to call us and we'd come get her. But I guess she's not about to ever listen to that, is she?"

"Maddy..." Jody rushed outside, with Elliot close behind.

"Don't call me that!" the girl shouted. "I told you that!"

"Sorry," Jody caught herself with regret. "Mad...I know...sorry."

Mad relaxed, almost smiled, then continued twisting the tire swing several times around in order to ride out the fast spin of the unwinding.

"Mad," Jody spoke gently, but firmly, "you really need to let Elliot or me to give you a ride down here. It's not safe, your walking the road like that."

"No car passed me on my way here this morning," she said.

"Mad, please listen to us," Jody's voice sharpened.

The girl stopped the swing and gave her a somber look. "Don't be angry at me."

"Jody and me," Elliot tried, "we're both very worried about you because we care about you. We want you to be safe."

Mad looked at the both of them, totally missing the value of their words. "I'm safe here."

"Here, yes," Jody agreed, "but not—"

"Go ahead, swing and sing, Mad," Elliot surprisingly gave way to the child. "Just promise to let us know when you're ready to go back home and we'll take you. Okay?"

The girl said nothing.

"Say okay," Elliot ordered her. "Say it!"

"Okay," Mad said in the tiniest of voices.

Jody and Elliot went back to the office. Though Mad stayed in the yard, she retreated from swinging and rather now played quietly along the edge of the garden.

"I don't want her to be scared of us," Jody warned Elliot.

"She's not used to being disciplined. It's good for her."

Jody could relate to Mad's being a headstrong child. She'd been that way herself at that age. And she couldn't help thinking that maybe her own little girl, somewhere out there in the far and distant world, might likely be of the same nature.

When Don arrived at the motel, his spirit was noticeably down. Not at all the happy bridegroom anymore.

"First marital quarrel?" Elliot couldn't resist asking him.

Don picked up the stapler and shot aimless staples into the air. "Guess Nora's got a set mind of her own."

Elliot rescued the stapler away from him. "Most women do."

"No...no, Nora's only ever been sweet and agreeable until—"

"Marriage can definitely bring out the worst in a person," Elliot offered.

"What's she done?" Jody asked.

"Nothing!" Don said ahead of storming off to the back room.

The Way Forward

"The *bitch*!" Elliot raved.

Jody slugged him in the arm. "Shhh…he'll hear you."

Whether Don heard or not, he immediately returned to the front office, his pride wounded but ready to talk of Nora again. "She wouldn't even listen to my idea. Her mind just clamed shut and she went slamming out of the cabin."

"What idea?" Jody asked.

"Like it's any of your business," he snapped.

"Then why are we talking about it?"

"Maybe it's a man-to-man thing, huh, Don?" Elliot suggested. "Maybe you and I should take a walk. I was married once, a long time ago. It left me with a lot of weird insight that might be helpful to you."

Don was amused at first by him, but in the next moment he was taking him seriously. "Yeah, sure, what the heck. Let's take a walk."

Elliot flashed Jody a smug grin on his way out, insuring that he had one up on her in this matter.

She was alone to mind the motel. And to think. About Don and about Nora and about Mad. Also about her having begged Elliot to let her stay with him and how his negativity toward it surprised her. Too many unsettling things.

The Pinewood Motel, tucked into the woods, was supposed to be a refreshing new start for everybody. And it had been until lately. Until Mad showed up out of the blue like the rebirth of her own daughter. And Don showed up out of the blue with a wife. And Elliot turned down her request to move in with him.

Feeling a tension headache coming on, Jody wandered into the back room and went to stand at the door to check on Mad. She was on the tire swing again, singing again. When she started on *You Are My Sunshine*, Jody's headache turned into a heartache.

Chapter 6

"There's a phone message for you from Nora," Jody told Don when he got home fifteen minutes after she did that day.

"You're checking my phone messages?" he snapped.

"Sorry. It was blinking and I just thought maybe, since I live here too, that it could maybe be for me, but it wasn't."

"Huh, why didn't she call my cell phone?" He played the message.

Nora's voice was cold and quick. "I'm covering part of the evening shift for Max because Earl can't come in. I'll be home about seven-thirty or eight." Click.

Don stood staring at the phone as if he were thinking of strangling it.

"I'll cook," Jody offered.

"Not hungry," he said, and just like that he left again.

Jody realized that she wasn't hungry either and opted for a bowl of cold cereal for her supper.

After washing her one dish and spoon, she packed some clothes into a travel bag and left. Not only was it unfair for her to have to share such close quarters with Don and Nora, but she knew her being there was unfair to them as well.

"No, no…a thousand times *no!*" Elliot said when he opened his cottage door and found her standing there with a bag and a needy look on her face.

She didn't need a welcome, she just needed in. She pushed past him and dropped her bag on the kitchen floor.

"What part of no don't you understand?" he asked.

"I have no home. I don't belong there anymore."

"Give your sister-in-law a chance, will you, for pete's sake? Two days is not a chance. Go back."

The Way Forward

"We're friends, you and me. And you have two bedrooms. I won't get in your way."

It was hard to tell if Elliot's muffled moan indicated another no or possibly a weak yes.

It didn't matter. She took her bag into the extra bedroom and closed the door behind her.

* * *

Don stormed into Maxy's, intending to drag Nora home. By the hair, if necessary, like a caveman claiming possession of his woman. But when she actually looked happy to see him, smiled, and waved him over, he melted.

He took a stool opposite the counter from her. "Hi."

"What are you doing here?" she asked.

"If the wife doth not come home, the husband goeth where she is."

"From the bible?"

He shook his head no. "Book of reason."

"You *have* one?"

He leaned forth to give her a kiss. A couple guys sitting at a near table applauded. Don laughed, swiveled his stool and gave a bow.

Max came from the storeroom, toting a case of beer. "Hey, Don. Sorry about keeping your wife late tonight." He put the case down behind the counter and paused to observe the two of them. "I still can't believe you two are hitched."

Don and Nora together held up their left hands, displaying their wedding bands.

Max laughed. "Okay, I believe it, but I *don't*. Know what I mean?"

"It did happen pretty fast," Don acknowledged.

"Anyway, I got my phone calls and bookwork caught up now, thanks to Nora, so you can take her home if you'd like."

Don nodded. "I'd like."

"Me too," Nora said in the tone of pure readiness.

"Goodnight…" one of the customers cooed to them on their way out. "Sweet dreams…or whatever."

Don and Nora walked to where their cars were parked next to each other in the lot.

"You can leave yours here and we'll get it tomorrow," Don suggested.

Nora leaned against the fender of his car, crossing her arms and seeming in no hurry to leave just yet. "I'm sorry I left in a snit this morning."

Don raised his hands forgivingly. "You're an independent girl. I shouldn't have tried to rein you in."

"*Rein me in?*" She narrowed her gaze at him.

"I'd rather you quit the bar and work at the motel, but I didn't mean to sound demanding about it. It's totally your choice."

Nora uncrossed her arms and moved away from the car. "You mean…the choice being whether I make myself happy or *you* happy?"

Don sighed. "That's not what I meant."

"I know you…how bummed out you can get if you don't get your way about things."

He gazed up at the dimming sky for a moment before looking back at her. "Nora, I've never been married before. Give me a chance to grow into this, will you?"

"Are you regretting that we got married so fast?"

"Stop twisting everything I say around. I'm trying to say I love you and let's go home."

"Yeah…lets."

"I'm happy we got married quickly. We both knew what we wanted."

"Home," she said amidst a yawn.

"I've never felt so right about anything in my life."

"Both cars," Nora said.

"I love you."

"Love you, too."

Don got into his car and waited for her to get into hers. With Nora closely following, just for fun he didn't head straight for home. He circled the small town-square in the center of Main Street, which consisted of a patch of grass, two benches and a light post. Three times he drove around it, with Nora playing the game right behind him. He laughed and said aloud for only himself to hear, "This definitely shows who's got the lead, baby."

When they arrived at the cabin and entered, Nora asked where Jody was.

Wrapping his arms around her, Don said, "I don't know and I don't care. Long as I know where *you* are."

Giving him a seductive look, she said, "I'm right here, lover, as close as I can get to you."

"I can think of a way to get still closer," he said, directing her to the loft ladder.

"Sounds interesting," she responded eagerly. Only to add, "But first, just to make sure you've got my final word on it, I'm not giving up my bartending to work at the Pinewood."

Following her up the steps, with his hand against her butt to assist her climb, Don said, "We'll see…"

"I'm *not*!" she insisted, the final word spoken between them before they crawled into bed to make love.

Chapter 7

Elliot was up and out of his bedroom and in and out of the bathroom before it hit him that Jody was there. That she'd forced her way into his cottage last night and took the extra bedroom, as if she had a perfect right to it. Jody had a *way* of claiming what she considered to be her rights.

Not about to get caught running around in his underwear, Elliot quickly got dressed. Then started a pot of coffee. Then began thinking it strange that as of yet he hadn't heard a sound from Jody's room. *Jody's room.* Unbelievable. Talk about rights…it was his cottage, and she was his guest, and being concerned about her gave him the right to go in and check on her.

He went to her door, stopped, shook his head no and walked away. Then he went back, stood even closer to the door and whispered, "Jody…?"

When she didn't answer, he carefully opened the door and sneaked inside. She was a little lump beneath a mound of blankets. But was she breathing? Feeling like an overly cautious new father, he knew he wouldn't be totally sure if she was all right until…

"*What are you doing?*" Jody flipped over with a startle.

It was a toss up as to who was most shocked in that instant, he or she.

"Just…just checking…" he said.

"*Checking what?*"

Her dark hair was in a wake-up tossle, and a pajamaed shoulder was sticking out of the covers.

"To…to see if you were breathing," he said.

"I'm breathing!" she snarled.

"Sorry."

"Get out of here!"

"I'm getting," he said, backing his way out of the shade-darkened room.

Returning to the kitchen, he wasn't sure now if *he* was breathing. He held a hand on his chest. His heart was beating rapidly. Stupid, going in there. Stupid, stupid, stupid. *Jeez*, what was he thinking? What was *Jody* thinking? On the other hand, she'd been really upset when she'd shown up last night and might've harmed herself in there. He doubted it, but couldn't afford to put anything past her.

Elliot convinced himself that he'd done the right thing, going in to check on her. He would never have forgiven himself if she'd done something foolish to herself and to save embarrassment he'd failed to save her.

Man, he was already feeling the hefty responsibility he was assuming by taking Jody in. At the same time, the other side of his brain was telling him that hadn't he *always* felt a special responsibility toward her? And yet again, this was different in that now they were sharing a house, and he had to wonder how responsible was *that?* Confusing. Jody could confuse him to no ends.

He tapped the side of the coffee maker, as if that would hurry the brewing. He needed caffeine desperately.

* * *

Jody dressed, left her room, spent some time in the bathroom, then joined Elliot in the kitchen. "Mind telling me what that checking thing was about?"

"Oatmeal or eggs?" he asked, standing with his back to her.

"Toast and jam."

"*Jeez*, you'd think this was a restaurant with choices."

"I've been here enough to know you have toast and jam on hand."

"That won't stick to your ribs."

Jody sat down to the table. "Aside from your so-called thoughtfulness of coming into my room to see if I was alive, you really hate that I crashed here, don't you?"

He turned to face her. "I only hate that you felt you *had* to crash here."

"You don't know what it's like at Don's cabin. Excuse me…Don and Nora's cabin. Nora's taken over the kitchen like I don't even exist. But she lets me help. She and Don, they're always grabbing each other. Mainly, I've lost my bedroom to them. Not that I'd ever want it back now after—"

"Okay, I get the picture. You're like the fifth wheel there now, aren't you"

"Exactly."

"I can imagine your discomfort," Elliot said sympathetically. "I guess, if you had to run, it's better you wound up here than who knows where."

Jody smiled. "I suppose I could have oatmeal."

"Good girl."

"Elliot..." Jody said wondrously.

"Yeah?"

"If I stay here, in my own room of course, you're—"

"Stay?" Elliot gasped.

"—not going to be mothering me, are you?"

"No. White sugar or brown?"

"Brown."

"Good girl."

"Because you're doing that now," she told him.

As he stuck her oatmeal into the microwave, he again questioned, "Stay?"

"You didn't think this was just a one-night stand, did you?"

The phone rang and Elliot grabbed it, answering questions in quick, short responses. "Yeah. She is. Right. Okay."

He hung up, telling Jody, "Your brother was looking for you."

"Like he cares," she scowled.

Elliot brought the bowl of oatmeal to her. "You're jealous of Nora, aren't you? That's really what all this is about."

"No!"

"Jealous!" He poured the milk onto her cereal for her and added a couple of spoonfuls of brown sugar to it.

Jody crossed her arms and gave a huff. "I'm...I'm just upset that my brother is so dumb."

Elliot sighed. "Oh, Jody, when are you going to cut your apron strings to him? He's a big boy. Let him live his life. Be glad, at least, that he's back in your life after he'd been gone for eight years prior to last summer."

"And what about Mad?" she said, switching the subject.

"She can't be your problem either, Jody. Come on...quit looking for trouble."

She started eating her oatmeal. "My coming to stay with you...do you consider *that* looking for trouble."

"Hell, yes," he said behind a forgiving grin.

It was sweet, Jody thought, how Elliot's attempts to act tough only seemed to enhance his teddy-bear appeal. She smiled, left her chair, went around the table to where he sat, and kissed the top of head.

"What's that for?" he asked.

"For letting me stay here."

"Did I actually *say* that you could?"

"Yes, I think so."

"Like your thinking beats my not saying?"

"We need to get ready for work," she said.

"Finish your oatmeal first."

"Yes, mommy."

Before they left the cottage, Don arrived. He knocked then entered on his own, as if he couldn't wait to blast Jody. "Just what do you think you're doing, spending the night here?"

"Sleeping," she replied smugly.

Don slid his look to Elliot.

Elliot held up his hands in defense. "Separate bedrooms. Her idea, not mine. I mean, about coming here. The separate bedroom thing, I agreed to that once I realized she was staying. I mean, things are cool here, Don. Really."

"Anyway," Jody confronted her brother, "it took you until this morning to worry about where I might be spending the night?"

Don sank onto a chair. "*Women.* Now I've got two of them to deal with."

"You no longer have to deal with me," Jody established. "I've freed you of that."

"How about you just take some time to adjust to married life," Elliot consoled him, "and leave Jody to me. You can owe me for the favor."

Don laughed, "I'm sure my dues will be immensely high."

"Ungodly," Elliot verified.

Jody punched him in the arm.

Don hung his head, gathering his thoughts ahead of telling his sister, "I'm sorry I took off again on you without a warning. It was selfish of me."

"It was, and I accept your apology."

He stood up and gave Jody a hug.

"Hey, I'm the injured party here," Elliot whined, still clutching his arm. "More like I'm the one who needs a hug."

Don turned and gave him a hug also. "I'm sorry my sister slugged you."

"Thanks," Elliot said.

The three of them, standing there in the cottage kitchen, shared a burst of mood-lifting laughter.

"Anyway," Don began in another moment," Nora and I will be looking for a real house before long. When her son comes to—"

"Son?" Jody shrieked.

"Yeah. Kenny. He's been living with his dad, Nora's ex. But she wants him back with her. And he wants to be back with her. And we want to make a real home for him."

"*Son?*" Jody repeated, stuck there.

"You knew about him before you guys got married?" Elliot questioned.

The Way Forward

"Of course."

"How old is the kid?" Elliot asked.

"Fifteen."

"Fifteen?" Jody exclaimed. "Nora has a *fifteen-year old kid?* Just how old *is* this woman you married?"

"Nora's thirty-six."

"Wow, almost my age," Elliot said, as if he pitied her. "But she looks damn good, more like *twenty-six*."

"She had Kenny when she was twenty-one," Don established.

"You married an older woman?" Jody said, disapprovingly.

"A few years is meaningless," Don responded. "On the other hand, there's quite a *few* years difference between you and Elliot, right?"

"But we're not married," Jody stated.

"Exactly!" Don said, with reference to their having spent the night together.

Elliot was quick to defend it. "Things were cool. Two bedrooms. No hanky pank, believe me. You and Nora qualify for hanky pank, at least till her son shows up. But not us, I assure you. Really."

While Don stood staring at his sister, Elliot opened the door, saying. "Time to get to work. At least for some of us. Don, go talk to your old logging boss if you want to. That might very well be a good idea for you."

As the three of them walked down the path to the motel, the delicate voice of Mad's singing wafted through the trees.

"What's that?" Don asked.

"Mad," Jody said.

It was hardly enough of an answer to him, and he secondly asked Elliot, "*Who?*"

"There's this little girl, Madison, who lives down the road from us. She comes here to swing on the tire swing and sing. Jody and I told her not to walk along the highway alone like that, but she does it anyway. Unfortunately it seems she's poorly supervised at home."

"We're not sure yet what to do about her," Jody added.

"Do?" Don questioned.

They reached the yard behind the motel and stopped at the sight of the girl swinging and singing. She didn't notice them right away and thus continued her song.

"Someone needs to take responsibility for this child," Elliot explained to Don. "Jody thinks that's us."

Mad stopped singing and swinging when she saw the three people approaching her.

"Mad…" Jody said, "I'd like you to meet my brother, Don."

The girl left the tire, stood as tall as a seven-year old could, and smiled cutely at him. "Hi."

"Hi," Don said, seeming immediately smitten by her. "What was that great song you were singing?"

"*You Are My Sunshine*, stupid," Jody razzed him for not knowing the classic.

Mad giggled. "Except not with the word *stupid*."

"Yeah," he newly considered, "I guess I maybe heard the song somewhere in my past. An oldie, right?"

"My mom used to sing it to me," Mad said.

Jody knew she was supposed to feel good toward Mad's saying that, but somehow it struck her with an unexpected ache of jealousy. She started for the back door of the motel office, leaving the girl with, "We'll be inside if you need us."

And Elliot, pointing his finger at Mad, left her with, "You're not to go back down that road alone. You come and get one of us to walk you or drive you when you're ready to go. Okay?"

She gave a mere nod, that probably only meant maybe, then draped herself back into the tire opening.

As the three adults went inside, behind them the sweet little voice began again on the sunshine song.

"*Lawdy, Miss Clawdy!*" Benjamin exclaimed at the sight of Don walking into the office with Jody and Elliot. "I hear you got yourself married."

"Yes, I did," Don replied proudly.

"Good for you. Congratulations."

"Thanks. So how you doing, Benj?"

"Not as good as you, I guess. I mean, I ain't got married or anything. But yeah, I'm doing all right. Keeping your motel available to night callers. Though ain't many come in the night."

Elliot motioned to the back. "How long's Mad been out there?"

"Half hour or so," Benjamin said. "Cute kid. Sure can sing. Been enjoying the listen. You said she lives down the road?"

"She's not suppose to come down here alone," Jody said. "We told her to call us and we'd give her a ride, but she just keeps coming by herself."

"Well, that ain't safe," Benjamin agreed.

"Try and tell her that," Elliot said.

Benjamin gathered together the few belongings he always brought. "Guess I'll be leaving. Good seeing you back, Don. Jody, Elliot…see ya later."

"Later," Elliot said.

After Benjamin left, Don went to the back door to take a last look out at the little girl in the tire swing. Then shaking his head and smiling, he took off to go see about getting his old logging job back.

Jody sank onto the stool behind the counter and gave a sigh.

Elliot asked, "Is that a good sigh or a bad sigh?"

"A confused one."

"Ah…"

"I can't believe Don wants out of the motel business already?"

"I don't think it's so much that he wants out of the motel business, as that he really misses his previous job."

"Yeah, I suppose."

Elliot laughed. "He sure got riled about your having spent the night at my place, didn't he?"

"But you saw how long it lasted, right? He's got enough going on in his life right now without spending time worrying about me."

"You sound sorry."

Jody rolled her eyes. "Yeah, right." Feeling the need to go check on Mad again, she left the counter and headed for the back room.

Elliot moved quickly enough to catch her by the arm to stop her. "About Mad…it doesn't do us any good to keep questioning the kid. If we really want to help her, we've got to find another way around this situation."

Jody smiled at him. "*We?*"

He smiled back at her. "Yeah…sure…do I have a choice?"

"We make a good team, don't we?"

"Yeah, I guess. Even before we started living together."

Chapter 8

Before Don went to see about retrieving his old logging job, he decided to first go back to the cabin and tell Nora that his decision about doing it was definite and to also let her know that Jody was okay.

She wasn't there. He checked his watch. It was eight forty-five. Okay, sure, Maxy's opened at nine and she was undoubtedly on her way there. He must have just missed her. Time had gotten away from him, talking with Jody and Elliot.

For the way he'd rushed over to Elliot's a while ago, angered over finding that Jody'd spent the night there, he'd since cooled off with the realization that he needn't have worried so about her. His kid sister wasn't exactly a kid anymore. And Elliot, he reminded himself, was a good guy who could surely be trusted to treat her with respect.

He went back to his car, deciding he'd go talk to Nora at the bar. What he wanted to tell her couldn't wait until tonight. Plus he could really use her support before going to talk to Jim. Nine was an early opening for a bar, but with a cook in the kitchen, breakfast was available to Myre dwellers, Pinewood guests, and passing-through travelers.

When Don arrived at Maxy's he found one of its regular customers already sitting at the bar. He'd seen her in there often, day and night.

"Hey, Claire, how's it going?"

The woman shrugged and made a nasty face. "Same shit as usual."

Don gave her a thumbs-up. "Gottcha."

Nora looked suspicious of his untimely visit, especially as he approached her saying, "I came to tell you a decision I made."

She turned up a half smile, guessing, "You want a divorce."

He stretched across the counter to kiss her.

"Oh please!" Claire, from just down the way, exclaimed. "I'm eating my breakfast here."

Don settled back from Nora. "I've definitely decided to try getting my old logging job back. I'm on my way now to talk to Jim."

"And you're here to try and—"

"No. No, I'm here to tell you that no matter what I think, you have to make your job decision on your own. And I support that."

"No kidding?"

"No kidding," he verified.

"You're letting me off the hook? Why?"

He grinned. "Because you're so damn good in bed."

"Pal…eeze!" Claire bellowed.

"Actually," Don told Nora, "I'm a little nervous about going back to Jim like this and I was hoping for your support."

"As long as I don't need to be your replacement at the Pinewood, you have it. I think I also believe that you're more suited to logging than moteling."

"Really?" he responded, feeling as happy as a kid on Christmas.

"Really," Nora laughed then automatically went about making a refill for Claire.

Setting the new glass before her and taking the empty one away, she asked in a bartender's chatty manner, "So what's on your agenda today, Claire?"

The woman pulled her cardigan sweater tighter about her thin shoulders. Having finished her breakfast plate, she took a sip of her fresh drink. "So far I drove my granddaughter to her new hangout, where she'll spend a good part of the day swinging. Crazy, I know. She usually walks, but she begged me to drive her today. So what the heck, it's in the opposite direction of here and I drove a little out of my way. Guess it ain't that big a deal. And later today I'm—"

"Wait!" Don's interest suddenly perked at the woman's chatter. "Your granddaughter…her name wouldn't happen to be Mad, would it?"

The woman swiveled her stool toward him. "How'd you know that?"

"I met her this morning. Out behind the Pinewood Motel. She loves that tire swing. I'm a third owner of the place. My sister Jody introduced me to Mad."

Claire gave a huff. "Jody, yeah! I met her and Edmund and—"

"Elliot," Don said.

"Whatever. They're getting pretty nosey about things, those two. Things concerning Mad. Seems they think I can't handle the kid. But I'll tell ya…I been handling Mad for over a year now. Ain't a bad job. I do okay. And the kid does okay. But I suppose maybe I am a little old for it. And I suppose maybe she needs her mother more 'en me. But the fact is…her mother don't seem to need her."

"How come you never mentioned your family to me before?" Nora retorted.

Claire shrugged. "Subject never came up."

"What kind of bartender *are* you?" Don razzed Nora.

Claire narrowed her gaze at the couple. "I been watching you two become closer and closer. Wasn't surprised to hear you got married. You two…" She wagged her finger at them, "you'd make great parents for Mad. How'd you like to adopt her?"

"Whoa!" Don reacted quickly. "That's something you don't just throw out there like an unwanted piece of furniture."

Nora was nodding in agreement. "Claire, this is sad. You need to make your daughter come back and take responsibility for her child."

"Ha," Claire pooh-pooed the idea.

"And speaking of families and what's best for them," Nora turned the matter inward, "as you know I have a son and he—"

"Yeah, you've mentioned Kenny to me a couple times," Claire acknowledged.

"Well, he's going to be coming here to live with Don and me."

"Way it should be," Claire said, her eyes twinkling at that idea in addition to her own. "So…how'd you like a little sister for Kenny? Seriously!"

Don and Nora exchanged looks.

"She's a darling little girl," Claire continued. "Nobody could ask for a more darling child. It's not that I don't love her, but you two could be a real mother and father to her. I…I think she needs that."

Don couldn't believe how this woman was so casually, yet seriously, trying to give her granddaughter away. People just don't do that. But then he supposed Claire, all in all, was not your average person. Maybe her heavy drinking habit corroded her better senses, and he knew the concern coming over him was as much for her as it was for her granddaughter.

Suddenly he noticed Nora giving him a very heart-tugging, maternal look. Tilting his head to one side, he in response gave her a look of warning. "Let me get used to having one kid first, okay?"

Don kissed her again, said good-bye to Claire, then headed for logging country.

*　　*　　*

Mad had already been playing in the motel back yard for hours before coming into the office to let Jody know, "My grandma gave me a ride here this morning."

The Way Forward

Jody looked up from her bookwork behind the counter. "She did? Good. I like that much better than your walking."

"She told me it was a one-time thing."

"Oh."

"What cha doing?" Mad asked, with childlike curiosity.

"Working on some records."

"Could you maybe play one for me?"

Jody laughed. "Not that kind of records. Book records, information that keeps track of our motel business. Wanna take a look?"

Mad eagerly peered over the counter as Jody turned the ledger around to her. Mad's facial expression went blank. "I don't understand it."

Jody laughed again. "Sometimes I don't either."

"It's going to be lunchtime pretty soon, isn't it?" Mad figured.

Jody looked at the clock. "You're right. Want me to take you back to your grandma?"

"I don't think she's home yet. She said she had a lot of stuff to do today."

"She left you alone? Like for the day?"

"I'm not alone. I'm with you and Elliot."

Hearing his name brought Elliot out from the back room.

Jody told him, "I think Mad will be joining us for lunch today."

"All right!" he disbursed enthusiastically. "And what would little Madam like…lobster, steak, frog legs?"

Mad giggled. "I like peanut butter sandwiches."

"Me too," Jody said. "And since Elliot has the makings at his cottage, I don't think he'd mind if you and I walked down there and indulged."

Mad jumped up and down. "I'll be happy to see your house, Elliot. Is it really just down that little path out back?"

He nodded. "It's there. Hope you like *creamy* peanut butter, 'cause that's the kind I have."

"I do."

"Give me about ten minutes, okay?" Jody told her.

"I'll be swinging."

As Mad disappeared, Elliot questioned Jody. "*My* house? You live there, too, now, it seems."

She smiled at that. "Yeah, I do, don't I."

"Yeah, you do," Elliot said in his own amazement. "Like, I mean, feel free to invite who you want whenever."

He returned to the back room. Left alone with her thoughts, Jody found herself feeling pretty happy right now. About Don, about Mad, about Nora, about Elliot, about almost everything. She even began pleasantly thinking back to that one rainy evening last fall, at Elliot's motel in Winona, when she and he sat in the office, sipping wine and sharing some deep talk. Then suddenly, to the amazement of both of them, they were kissing. It went no further than that, nor had there ever been, since then, another such incident between them. But it had thrown an unsettling curve into their relationship that would always be there for them to wonder about.

And now they were going to be living together. Not as lovers, but as buddies. How strange was that? Only that she needed a place to live, and Elliot happened to have a place. That was it. Later today, or for sure tomorrow, she would go back to Don's place to pick up more of her stuff, making her move to the cottage official.

"It's raining! It's finally raining!" Elliot cheered, watching it coming down outside his cottage windows that evening after dinner. "Man, do we need this!"

Lightning flared, followed by a clap of thunder. He joined Jody in the living room and sat on the other end of the couch from her. "Scared?" he asked of her curled-up-tight position.

She grinned. "No...I feel perfectly safe with you."

He grinned back at her. "Are we talking thunderstorm or sex?"

She asked him, "Do you feel safe with *me*?"

"No," he laughed. Then seriously confessed, "I want to tell you that I never lived with another woman since my divorce many years ago."

Jody looked at him in awe. "Why are you telling me this now? Or at all?"

"Just making conversation."

"Does this mean..." she began slowly and carefully, "that you do, now, with my living here, consider yourself to be living with a woman?"

At first he looked at her as if maybe he'd never even considered her to be a *woman*. Then he side-stepped his answer. "We're uh...not sleeping together. And we won't be."

Jody picked up the remote and clicked on the TV.

*　　*　　*

When Don got home to the cabin that evening, he found a note from Nora saying she'd be home late but to wait up for her because she'd be bringing a surprise. He was both disappointed and intrigued. But deciding not to dwell on it one way or the other, he fixed himself some supper then got comfortable before the TV.

The Way Forward

It'd been a hard, but good, day. Jim had been glad to see him, rehired him on the spot, reissued him a hard hat and some equipment, and put him immediately to work.

Though his body ached now from a type of physical labor he hadn't been used to for some time, he accepted it like a well-earned reward.

During a run of commercials he took a hot shower. It soothed his muscles and stilled his wired brain. Nice…but the best of his well being would be when Nora got home. She would give him a good back massage and a lot more. He was anxious for her. He checked the time. It was after nine now and he couldn't help starting to worry. There wasn't much on TV to interest him, but he kept it on to pass the time.

Finally there came the sound of a car pulling up outside. Then the welcomed sound of the cabin door opening.

Nora wasn't alone. There was a gangly teenaged boy at her side. *Kenny.*

Don rose off the couch, forcing a smile. Okay, he was happy about her son coming to live with them, but he just wasn't expecting him quite this soon. Hell, he and Nora were still on their honeymoon. And they hadn't yet started looking for a house. And she'd never mentioned this morning about…

"Honey," Nora said, drawing him out of his state of shock, "this is Kenny. Kenny, this is Don, your step dad."

The guys stepped forth to meet each other with a handshake.

"Hi, Kenny," Don managed to put some warmth in his voice. "Welcome."

"Hi," was all the boy said, though with readable pleasure.

Don shifted his look to Nora and laughed. "Your note said you were bringing home a surprise. Man, this is sure a big one."

"Five ten, to be exact," Kenny stated.

Don leveled his hand comparatively between the heights of both of them. At Kenny's being two inches shorter than he, Don concluded teasingly, "Yep…you're almost a man."

"I left work early," Nora began to explain, "came home for a couple things, left you the note, then went to pick him up at the Duluth airport. The plane ended up being late. I hope you didn't mind my keeping this as a surprise."

Don's attention remained on Kenny. "Hungry?" he asked him.

Before Kenny could answer, Nora declared, "He's always hungry. He'll reach six foot before we know it."

"Come on," Don said, motioning to the kitchen side of the room. "I'll heat something up for you. There's leftovers from my supper. How about you, Nora?"

"No thanks, I'm fine. What kind of leftovers?"

"Chili with chopped up hot dogs, onions and cheese."

Nora moaned.

Kenny cheered, "Awesome!"

Minutes later, as the boy sat at the table eagerly spooning up his enjoyable supper, he glanced about at everything to be seen from that one spot. Eventually he asked, "Where will I be sleeping?"

"Couch," Don said.

"And you guys?" Kenny asked.

Don motioned to the ladder.

Kenny's eyes followed it up to the railed loft. "Oh."

"We'll be getting a bigger house in time," Don assured him.

"My dad's trailer is smaller than this," Kenny stated.

"Then welcome to my mansion," Don quipped.

"*Our* mansion," Nora corrected him.

"*Our* mansion," Kenny included himself.

"The three of us, yes," Don verified, getting a slight catch in his throat.

How ironic, he thought, that Jody had almost no more than moved out and now Kenny was moving in. Like a trade off. Not to be considered a better or worse one, only that he and Nora still weren't alone.

After getting Kenny settled with a pillow and a blanket and the TV remote, Don and Nora went upstairs. As soon as they snuggled together in bed and exchanged a few kisses, he told her, in a whisper, about how well his return to his logging job went. She was happy for him, though he supposed she was mostly happy that she wasn't going to be his replacement at the Pinewood. And he supposed that was okay.

Don saw Kenny as a nice kid. He'd liked him right off and knew they'd get along well. It's just that…with Nora in his arms and Kenny right below them downstairs, he felt the sacrifice of losing their privacy. Thus kissing and hugging and sweet whispers would be the extent of their lovemaking tonight. And he supposed that, too, was okay. For now.

Chapter 9

"I didn't know he was coming here so soon," Don spoke in a low voice to Nora, as the two of them ate breakfast together in the kitchen the next morning.

She looked over at Kenny, still asleep on the couch. "He couldn't stand it at his dad's place any longer. He'd just been waiting for the right time to move here with me."

"And this was it?" Don asked.

"The timing…yeah, I know."

"I would've rather you'd told me ahead of time instead of surprising me."

Nora lowered her gaze sheepishly.

"You didn't think I'd like the idea, did you?" he said. "It wasn't so much about surprising me as it was about your getting Kenny here before I could react to the idea."

Nora met eyes with him again. "I knew it was kind of soon. Sooner than either you or I planned. But when he called me with such desperation, I just said yes, come."

Giving her a slow, soft smile, Don told her, "I guess you haven't known me long enough yet to know that I'm not a monster."

"You're not a monster."

"Thank you."

"But you're a newly-married man who—"

"Yeah, things are happening fast, that's for sure. But above it all, I love you. And Kenny's a part of you. And heck, I think I'm really going to like having a stepson."

Don left his chair, went to stand behind Nora, bent down and wrapped his arms around her. With a slightly-wounded ego, he whispered, "I just didn't think the honeymoon would be over so soon."

She stood up, turning directly into him. "Are you kidding me? It's far from over, lover."

Don made a flash glance at the couch. The kid was still out, thus he took advantage of it and shared a deep, honeymoon kiss with his wife.

"As long as we can sneak moments like this," Nora sighed as they parted.

"I'm a good sneak," Don assured her.

"Good. Me too."

They finished their breakfast, and Nora remained at the table with another cup of coffee while Don got ready for work. His job began long before hers.

Before he left the cabin he stood for a moment looking at Kenny. The boy was still sound asleep, understandably wiped out from yesterday's travels.

"So what's he going to do around here all day alone?" Don asked Nora.

"I noticed your bike out along side the cabin and took the liberty of telling him he could use it. Okay?"

"Sure."

"I gave him directions to Maxy's, if he should want to come hang out with me. Also to the Pinewood Motel."

Don raised his eyebrows to the latter.

Nora went to the door with him. "I thought he might apply for your replacement job there."

Holding Nora in his arms, Don needlessly reminded her, "He's fifteen."

"He could handle the job, believe me. He's a good worker. He's already had several jobs. I mentioned the possibility of the motel to him and he's excited about it. Let's give him the chance, okay?"

Okay," Don said, ahead of kissing his wife good-bye. Then he started out the door, insuring, "I suppose Elliot will know what to do with him."

*   *   *

Elliot looked up from the desk when the motel office door opened and a young boy entered. "Sorry," he quipped, "we don't let rooms to minors...no matter how cute their girlfriend might be."

"I'm not here about a room," the boy responded. "I'm here about a job."

Elliot put down his pen and went around the counter to get a closer look at the prospective employee. "How old are you, anyway? And where did you—"

"I...I'm sixteen...and...my name's Kenny...and I'm Don Mitchell's son."

Elliot jumped to the truth of it. "You're *fifteen* and you're *Nora's* son and I don't like liars."

The Way Forward

Kenny's eyes glimmered with surprise. "Sorry. I just really want this job. I didn't think you already knew about me."

Elliot chuckled. "Watch out for the wisdom of your elders." He offered his hand to the boy and they shook. "Yeah, I've already heard of you, Kenny. I'm Elliot. You probably haven't heard of me."

"Just your name."

"So Don sent you here, did he?"

"No, my mom."

Elliot glanced out the window at the parking lot. "How'd you get here?"

"Bike. Don's bike. I'm living at the cabin with him and my mom now."

"That was quick."

"Excuse me?"

Elliot shook his head, still amazed at the whole situation. "Nothing. Nice meeting you, Kenny. Really."

"I just arrived last night."

"Quick," Elliot said again. "And you're already looking for a job."

"I need a summer job, yeah. My mom said you could probably use someone."

Jody came into the office, yawning and coming around to the new day much slower than Elliot had. She was surprised, finding someone with him.

Motioning to her with the sweep of his hand, Elliot told Kenny, "Your Aunt Jody."

"Kenny?" Jody looked at him with new eyes.

"Yes," he said. "Nice to meet you. You look a lot like your brother, except that you're a girl."

"And you look a lot like your mother," she said, "except that you're a boy."

"*Families,*" Elliot drawled. "I have absolutely no one that looks like me."

"Thank goodness," Jody teased.

"I'm applying for a job," Kenny said.

"Don sent you?"

Kenny shook his head. "My mom."

"How'd you—?"

"He biked," Elliot explained his transportation. "Don's bike."

"He gave me permission," Kenny was quick to assure her.

"How about you step outside for a few minutes," Elliot suggested to him, "so Jody and I can discuss your possible employment here. Take a look around the grounds. Take into consideration that if we do hire you, one of your duties might include pulling some of those nasty weeds out there."

"Okay," Kenny said, departing affably.

"So whatd'ya think?" Elliot asked Jody when it was just the two of them in the office.

"Isn't he a little young?"

"I like him."

Jody raised her eyebrows and tilted her head to one side.

"The Pinewood's a family business," Elliot made an allowance. "Kenny's family. That makes it okay. I mean since it's obviously okay with his stepdad and hopefully okay with his Aunt Jody..."

She gave a short laugh. "Will you stop with that Aunt Jody stuff." She glanced through the front window, watching Kenny stroll around the edge of the parking lot, checking out the flowerbeds. "This is just so weird, suddenly having a nephew out of the blue. Even weirder, Don's getting married out of the blue."

"Life is weird," Elliot justified. "And blue's not such a bad color."

Jody smiled. "I think I'm liking Kenny a whole lot faster than I liked Nora right off."

"Good." Elliot clapped his hands together and headed for the door, as if that were all it took to establish the boy was hired. "I'll invite him back in so we can tell him."

"Wait," Jody stopped his opening the door. "Look...Mad just arrived. The two of them, she and Kenny, are talking. Let's give them a moment."

Elliot was just as interested, seeing the two young people together. "Kinda look like a brother-sister thing, don't they?"

"Or cousins," Jody said. "Like since Kenny belongs to Don now, if Mad belonged to me they'd be cousins. Right?"

Elliot felt a familiar ache in his gut. He looked back at Jody's pitiful and reoccurring down side. "Come on...get those stars out of your eyes. Mad is not yours. Don't even do a what-if on that."

"I'm just saying—"

"I know what you're saying and what you've been thinking all along since meeting her. And it's not healthy."

Jody hung her head, speaking to him as if she were speaking to the floor. "She belongs to Claire, and to a mother who is out there somewhere, and not to me. I know that. I just...I just get to thinking beyond that sometimes."

Elliot gave her a playful rap on the noggin. "Stop it, okay?"

She remained looking down, standing in silence.

Elliot opened the door, called hello to Mad and invited Kenny to come back inside.

The boy came into the office, looking nervous over the decision he faced.

Elliot purposely let him sweat it out for a few long moments, pacing about the room under the boy's intense watch. Then he stopped directly before him, saying, "You're hired."

"Really?" Kenny exclaimed, as though he were five rather than fifteen.

"Yes," Jody verified. "And while Elliot shows you around and fills you in on things, I'm going to excuse myself to run an errand."

Elliot gave her a questioning look as to what that might be.

"I'm going to go talk to Claire," she explained. "I *have* to."

Claire…yes, that woman needed to be talked to, Elliot agreed to that all right. He only wished he were available to go with her. He worried at how Jody usually pushed way beyond need. But he let her go. He had a new employee to train in. "Ready to work?"

"Yes, Sir," Kenny said.

"You can just call me boss," Elliot told him, stretching his height to its max.

* * *

Though Claire wasn't particularly receptive to Jody's visit, she nevertheless invited her in and motioned her into the living room. Then she brought in a plate of cookies, of which Jody took one, and offered to pour her a glass of whisky, of which Jody declined.

Out of politeness, Jody took a bite of her cookie. Store-bought and stale, she set the rest of it on a side table. So much for being polite. "Where's Mad's mother?"

Claire shrugged her bony shoulders. "New York somewhere, last I knew."

"Why isn't Mad with her?'

"Because she's with me. Because her living with me works better than her living with her mother."

"Does she have a father?" Jody asked. "I mean…where might he be?"

Claire laughed. "He's even more out of the picture than Susan is."

"Susan? Your daughter's name?"

"He might be in Timbuktu, for all I know," Claire answered first about Mad's father. Then, "Yes, Susan, that's her name."

"Do you have actual custody of Mad?"

Claire's face tightened into a frown. "You ain't from Social Services, are you?"

"No. Look, Claire…it appears to be, from Elliot's and my point of view, that Madison just might be a bit too much for you to handle properly."

"Is that so?"

"Possibly."

"She's a good kid. And yes, I do have custody. And no, she ain't no trouble to me at all."

"You drink!" Jody charged the woman. "You drink a lot, don't you?"

"Some. I drink some."

"And you let Mad roam around on her own, don't you?"

"She goes to your motel to swing, that's all. If you don't want her there, I'll—"

"She's welcome there. We love having her there. It's just that it's not safe to let her walk that distance down the road by herself. Anyone could easily pick her up."

Claire gave it some brief thought. "Ain't nothin' happened to her so far."

Jody was enraged. "*So far*? Like you're going to wait until something bad happens before you take this seriously? I'm sorry, Claire, but it seems you're just not providing responsible care for Mad."

"I gave her a ride to your motel yesterday."

"One day."

The grandmother took a long chug from her whisky bottle ahead of saying, "You got no business judging me."

"Anybody who knows this situation would have the perfect right to judge it. Maybe it's time for you to admit it, Claire. And maybe it's time for you to admit that you might just need to get some help for yourself."

Claire sighed with a sadness Jody so far hadn't seen. "It didn't used to be this way."

"I'm sure," Jody gave her.

"I raised my Susan right. Then she got out on her own, moved away from here to Minneapolis, and her life went haywire. When she had Mad I thought she'd settle down, get back to her better morals and at least raise her own kid right. She tried. But eventually her drinking, mixed with all sorts of other problems, crashed in on her and she was forced into an institution to get straightened out."

"Rehab?" Jody questioned.

Claire nodded. "At that point, I have to say that I doubted anything would help Susan. But I hoped. And I got Mad dumped on me. Which was okay, I s'pose."

"Except that you, also, had a drinking problem."

"I lived alone a long time," Claire rationed, revealing a pathetic need to be understood. "Suddenly having a kid around here wasn't about to change my—"

"Being responsible for a child requires some change."

"Mad never seemed to mind my having a drink now and then," Claire said. "I never took it to extreme like I heard her mother did."

"Maybe you've never seen your granddaughter, or yourself for that matter, with a clear head."

The momentary glimpse of Claire's softer side was gone, and her voice now rose belligerently. "Why are you trying to make this your business?"

The Way Forward

"Because I care. And I'm concerned."

"You don't need to be."

"Is Susan still in rehab or is she out now?" Jody ventured on.

"I don't know. I'm not sure. I've lost track. What's the difference?"

"I'd like to contact her."

Claire got up from her chair and pointed to the door. "I think you'd better leave."

Jody stood, with a return of anger rising over the momentary compassion she'd felt toward the woman. "You have to know that this isn't the end of it."

When she got outside on the porch, she stopped and turned back to the resolute woman on the other side of the screen door. "I know you must love Mad, and I know you must think you're giving her the best care, but—"

Claire slammed the inside door in Jody's face.

Jody went to her car, got in, and left, disappointed that she'd failed her mission. She wanted to make Claire face her responsibility to Mad. But how quickly she found there was no talking logic to that woman. Plus how quickly it'd become evident that Claire's drinking was worse than suspected.

Well, okay then, Jody thought, recharging herself to the challenge…she'd just have to come up with a different approach. If it took a fight, it took a fight. Protecting Mad was a pretty strong incentive.

Chapter 10

Benjamin occasionally worked weekend night shifts instead of, and sometimes in addition to, his week night shifts. Elliot asked him to work this Saturday night so that he could take Jody out on the town.

"There's a bar and a grocery store," she reminded him of Myre's limitation. "Ah..." Elliot said thoughtfully, "but I hear they now have live music at Maxy's on Saturday's after eight. And after ten they sell dollar hot dogs."

"Sounds like heaven," Jody laughed.

"With a little imagination, yes."

He did the dishes by himself after supper, while Jody disappeared into her room for a long time. When she eventually came out, she was wearing something other than her usual jeans. She had on a beige skirt, a matching scoop-neck sweater, and sandals rather than tennis shoes. She was wearing makeup, and a sequined headband held her hair back from her face. Tonight she was more than cute. She looked absolutely beautiful.

"Something wrong?" she asked of his staring.

"No...uh, quite the contrary. You look great, Jody. I mean, like womanly great."

"Let's go." Shaking her head and mumbling to herself, she grabbed her purse and headed out of the cottage ahead of him.

They entered the Maxy's Bar to the lively sound of a four-piece country band playing in the back. The place was crowded. Elliot had to wonder where all these people came from. He searched for an empty table and was lucky enough to find one.

As soon as they sat down, a waitress approached them. It was *Nora*.

Jody was disturbed and didn't hesitate to show it.

"Hi, guys," Nora greeted them. "What can I get you?"

"I thought you only worked behind the bar," Elliot commented.

"If you were here more often," she laughed, "you'd see that I do everything everywhere around here."

"I'm impressed," Elliot said. "Beer."

"Same," Jody said for herself.

Nora gave her a skeptical look. "Now that we're sisters-in-law I know I should know your age, but—"

"I'm old enough," Jody sneered.

"She is, believe me," Elliot vouched for her. "Looks good for forty, doesn't she?"

Jody swatted him.

Before Nora started away, she paused to tell them, "Don's here. He's sitting at the bar. Been keeping company with Claire all evening. She—"

"Did you say Claire?" Elliot gasped.

Jody lifted off her chair, wrenching a look through the crowd in that direction.

"Yeah, Claire. I could be jealous, you know," Nora joked, "except that she's in her sixties and happens to be too good of a customer for me to make waves with."

As Nora left to fetch their drinks, Jody shrieked at Elliot, "It's her! Mad's grandmother."

"Imagine that," he said, also surprised but keeping his calm. "This is sure beginning to feel like family night, don't you think?"

Scanning the crowd from where she sat, Jody said, "I don't see Mad anywhere. Where's Mad?"

"I'm not seeing any kids in here," Elliot observed.

"But where is she? If Claire is here, where is Mad?"

"Probably home with a babysitter."

"Why does my gut say no to that—to Mad's having a babysitter?"

Elliot knew that when Jody started getting up, she was intending to go talk to Claire. *No, she shouldn't do that.* He pulled her back down, saving her grace and a possible barroom brawl. "Will you forget about the kid for just one evening? *Jeez*, so what if Mad is home alone? There's nothing we can do about it."

"How can you say that?" Jody shrieked like a child on the verge of crying. "I thought you cared about her."

"I do. I...I also care about you, and I just want you to unwind from that tight little brain of yours for one night."

"Impossible!" She broke away from his grasp and marched toward Don and Claire at the bar.

Elliot took after her.

"Hey, sis," Don greeted her approach. "Hey, Elliot."

Jody snatched up the glass he was nursing and took a sip from it. "Club soda."

"Yeah," Don scowled, "what'd ya think?"

"The worst. Sorry." She gave Claire, on the next stool, a stern look. "Where's Mad?"

Claire's eyes were glassy and her speech slurred. "At home."

"By herself?"

"I hope so. I told her not to allow anyone in."

Jody stuck her hands on her hips. "What is wrong with you!"

Nora saw them at the bar now and set their beers before them on the counter. Elliot grabbed his, but Jody ignored hers. She continued harping at Claire. "Mad's too young to be left alone. I could have the police on you."

Humored by that, Claire broke into a fit of laughter that set her teetering on her stool. "Wouldn't that be somethin'…like I'd do Mad better if I was in jail."

"Just maybe you would!" Jody argued.

"Simmer down," Don warned her. "Stop looking for trouble."

Jody poked her finger against Claire's shoulder. "She's the one who's trouble."

"Hey, you know what?" Don turned to Elliot, suggesting, "Why don't you get Little Miss Trouble out of here before somebody *throws* her out."

"Nobody's throwing me anywhere!" Jody bellowed, with ferocity now compromising her original loveliness.

"Come on," Elliot nevertheless urged her.

"No! I've got things to settle with Claire."

"Not much ever gets settled in a bar," he said.

"Mad's home alone?" she sought further verification from Claire. "You actually did leave her there alone?"

Claire stuck her tongue out at her.

"That's it, I'm outta here!" Jody decided on her own.

Elliot went with her, the two of them bumping into people, tables and chairs on their way out.

When Jody got to the car and realized it was Elliot's, not hers, she was glad he'd come with her. She turned, opening her hand to him. "Keys. You can get a ride home from Don later."

"Are you kidding?" he exclaimed. "Like I'm going to let you drive in that mood of yours? No, no…I'll drive."

She calmed down a bit and appreciated him with a warm smile. "Thanks."

The Way Forward

He opened the passenger-side door for her. "Our night out isn't exactly going the way I'd intended."

"Drive," she ordered him.

*   *   *

Jody was glad Elliot was doing this with her. She couldn't wait to get to Claire's house and check on Mad. She kept urging him to drive faster, and he kept telling her that he was but it didn't seem like it to her.

Minutes later they were there, and Jody was knocking on the front door. When it drew no response from inside, she called out to Mad. Still nothing.

A dim yellow light showed faintly through the window curtains. Surely Mad was in there. With her rising sense of urgency, Jody began pounding on the door.

Elliot grabbed her hand and stilled it. "That's enough. I think you've made our presence well known."

They waited on the porch, both of them emotionally edgy. Elliot cracked his knuckles while Jody gave endless little huffs.

Finally they detected a slight movement beyond the curtains.

"She's in there all right," Jody said. Stepping closer to the door again, she called out, "It's okay, Mad. It's me, Jody, and Elliot. Please open the door. You're not in trouble or anything. We need to talk to you."

"Please," Elliot added.

The lock clicked and the little girl appeared in the door opening. Despite the low light Jody could see that she'd been crying. "Oh…Mad…honey…"

When she tried putting her arms around her, the distraught child swiftly backed away.

This moment definitely called for a hug, and Jody felt badly that they couldn't connect. But she kept her distance, if that was what Mad wanted.

Mad didn't look better for it, she looked worse, and new tears were coming into her eyes. Maybe she needed a hug more than she knew. Jody decided to give it another try, and this time when she started to put her arms around Mad the girl was receptive and hugged her back. The two of them stood in their embrace for a time without talking.

Observing them brought Elliot's restrained anger to the surface. "So…" he concluded of Mad, "no one's staying with you and you've been scared shitless, right?"

She parted from Jody, wiped her eyes with her fist, and gave him a look that spoke for itself.

"*Jeez*," he said, shaking his head.

"How often does this happen?" Jody asked her.

Mad's lips quivered. "Am I going to get into trouble? Is my grandma?"

Jody gave her a reassuring smile. "No, not with me and Elliot around. We hate trouble. We...we just want to make things right. Because we don't think they are so right here, are they?"

Working hard at being brave, Mad slowly confessed, "It gets really quiet in the house when my grandma's not here. I think there might be a mouse sneaking around in the kitchen sometimes. But we never can catch him. He gets extra loud when my grandma's not here and when it gets dark outside."

"I told you," Jody said, "to call me and Elliot if you ever needed us. You've got the card I gave you, haven't you?"

"I...I think I lost it."

"Oh, Maddy..."

"Don't call me that!" the child cried.

"Sorry," Jody apologized. Then glancing at Elliot, she gave him a silent plea for help as to what to do next.

"How'd you like to come back to our place to spend the night?" Elliot asked Mad.

Jody loved his idea. It was perfect.

Mad, however, wasn't immediately fond of it. "I'm not allowed to...to go anywhere at night when Grandma's not here."

"And I'm saying that you're not allowed to stay here by yourself at night," Jody took it upon herself to overrule Claire. "Go pack your pajamas and toothbrush. You're coming with us."

Mad just stood there frozen and doubtful and scared in a whole new way.

Elliot squatted down to her level, looked her straight in the eye, and turned on his charm. "Please, Mad, it's okay. We'll leave a note for Claire and that'll make it okay. Really."

The girl went to pack, and Jody said a silent prayer of thanks in her head. Before she went to offer help to Mad, she thanked Elliot by giving him an affectionate jab in the arm.

"You're welcome," he said.

* * *

"That sister of yours is one crazy trouble maker, I've come to find out," Claire sputtered to Don, she with her whiskey and he with his club soda.

"Tell me about it," he laughed. But he was quickly solemn again toward the real matter at hand. "I think she went to check on Mad. And I think that was probably a good idea, Claire."

The Way Forward

"See what I mean?" Claire snarled. "She messes with things she oughtn't."

"Where's Mad's mother?" Don asked.

"Please...not you, too. Maybe I come here to forget a lota stuff, okay? I'd appreciate your...your respecting that."

"Looks like a serious conversation going on here," Nora observed, nearing the two of them from the inner side of the bar.

"She left her seven-year old granddaughter home alone," Don explained.

Nora was astonished. "Did you really, Claire? All the times you been coming here, you've been doing that? I didn't even know you *had* a granddaughter living with you till recently. Oh, Claire, you should have at least brought her with and—"

"I don't always drive so good on my way home," Claire justified.

Don and Nora exchanged looks of deepening concern.

"Jody and Elliot...they left to go check on Mad," Don told Nora.

"Good for them," she sighed with relief.

Claire studied the two of them. "You know what? It's like I was telling you guys the other day...you'd make great parents for Mad. I could give her to you, you know."

"You haven't yet told me where her mother is," Don said.

"Somewhere in New York," Claire replied matter-of-factly. Then slowly and sadly she added, "Somewhere's all I know. I've lost track. She...Susan... she *wanted* me to lose track."

"Susan?" Don verified. "Your daughter's name is Susan?"

Claire grimaced. "She's not as sweet as her name may presume. She's grown cold, that daughter of mine. Well...I suppose I have too, some, over the years...hard as life tends to become."

"What can we do?" Nora whispered for Don's ears only.

He shook his head and shrugged.

"What about your son?" Claire surprisingly asked Nora. "He old enough to stay home by himself?"

Before Nora could answer, Don quipped, "I suppose we could've had Jody and Elliot swing by and check on him also."

"He's old enough," Nora assured Claire. Then she made a face at Don for his silly comment. Then she smiled and leaned across the counter to get closer to him. "I think you kind of like Kenny already, don't you?"

Nodding exuberantly, he said, "I guess I always thought someday I might enjoy being a parent. I just didn't figure on starting out with a fifteen-year old kid."

"He likes you, too."

"Good. Teenagers can be dangerous if they hate someone."

"He's happy about getting a job at the Pinewood."

"Wait till he has to scrub a toilet."

"And you…you're really okay with me keeping my bartending job?"

"No, but I'm biting my tongue."

"Good." She drew herself still closer to him for a kiss.

"*Mush*," Claire sputtered at them. "Young love don't know much else but mush."

"That's right," Don took the disgrace well.

Chapter 11

Jody woke up Sunday morning feeling strange and illusory. It couldn't be real that she was in Elliot's spare bedroom and that she'd actually taken up residence with him. And how real was it that Don was married? And had a fifteen-year old stepson? Or that last night she'd rescued Mad away from being alone and frightened in her grandma's house. Or what did it mean that she couldn't help comparing Mad to what she could only imagine her own little girl to be like at this very time?

Still lying in bed, she closed her eyes and sought the peacefulness of falling back to sleep. She gave it ten minutes, but when it didn't come by then she got up, dressed, and quietly opened her door to the living room. Mad was asleep on the couch, snuggled deep beneath the blanket except for her forehead of bangs and her cute little nose.

Elliot was in the kitchen making coffee. He turned on Jody's approach and smiled at her. Neither spoke. It was one of those times when their minds seemed so connected to one another that words could not say more. It happened often in their relationship.

Jody sat at the table observing Elliot, wondering if they would ever become more than just friends. She really didn't know if she wanted them to be more. Nor did she know if Elliot wanted that. *Don't fix what ain't broke* was a saying that came to her mind whenever she pondered the possibility of something more between them. This was nice. This was enough. This was comfortable and secure.

When Elliot brought two mugs of coffee to the table and sat across from Jody, she finally broke the silence. "What are we going to do about her?"

"Mad." He met her concern knowingly.

"Yes."

Elliot chuckled. "I'm still not sure what I'm going to do about *you*."

She sipped some coffee. "We need a plan. Help me think of a plan, Elliot."

"Last time you told me we needed a plan, we handcuffed your brother and kidnapped him from his cabin up here and hauled him all the way back to down to Winona."

"It was a good plan."

"It was a hare-brained idea."

"It worked."

"Damned if it didn't."

"I couldn't believe you found a place to buy a real pair of handcuffs."

"Buying 'em wasn't the difficult part."

Jody laughed softly. "Don didn't much like being restrained in them, did he?"

"He put up a hell of a fuss in the back seat of my car."

"It was the only way we could've forced him home. We had to take drastic measures."

Elliot motioned toward Mad on the couch. "Another drastic measure?"

"I won't turn my back on her again."

Elliot's eyes narrowed. "Again? Jody, she's not the baby you gave up seven years ago. Come on, don't go sicko on me here."

"I know, but—"

"If you want to help Mad, do it because she's Madison and not some other little girl. Okay?"

Elliot was right.

It was fun when Mad woke up. She was bubbly and talkative and seemingly unfazed by last night's episode. She sat at the table in her pink polka-dot pajamas. The three of them exchanged simple chit chat and silly kids' jokes.

After breakfast, of pancakes that Elliot managed to make in the shape of mickey-mouse's head, Jody drove Mad home. On the way, she asked what her last name was.

"Windle," Mad said.

"Can you spell it for me?"

"W-I-N-D-L-E. My grandma has the same last name."

Jody gave her a sidelong look. "Your grandma, your mother, and you?"

"Yes."

When they got to Claire's house, Jody didn't go in with Mad. Maybe she should have, but she didn't want to get into a confrontation with the grandma at this particular time. Claire's car was there, so at least that was something to feel good about. *She hoped.*

"Thanks about last night," the girl said as she left Jody.

"You're welcome. We loved having you for a guest."

"Can I ask you something?"

"Sure."

"How come you and Elliot have different bedrooms?"

Jody was astounded that she would ask, let alone notice. "W-well…Elliot and I, we're not married."

"Oh," Mad seemed to easily accept that. Though she compared it with, "Once when I lived with my mom, she slept with a man she wasn't married to."

"Some day, when you're older," Jody began carefully, "we'll have a talk about this."

"Will we still know each other then…when I get older?"

Jody swallowed hard ahead of answering. "I think so. I hope so. Now go inside to your grandma. I'm sure she'll be happy to see you."

"She'll probably still be sleeping…" Mad said in a trailing-off voice as she walked to the house.

Jody was quiet and kept to herself when she returned to Elliot's place. But when her mind settled, she told him, "I have a lead, as to Mad's mother. I have both her first and her last names now and I know that she lives in New York."

"Good work, detective."

"So now I can try and search out her phone number."

"You couldn't get that as well from the kid?"

"I didn't want to be real obvious."

Elliot laughed.

Jody gave a sigh and flopped into an easy chair. "Okay…I guess I could've asked Mad. I guess I should've."

"Names in New York aren't exactly the most sufficient lead."

"Don't cut down my hopes."

"Sorry." Elliot perched on the arm of her chair. "I don't know, Jody… maybe we ought to report this situation to the officials who could check into Mad's welfare appropriately."

"*Appropriately*? Technically is how they'd handle it. Which is not always appropriate in my book." She gave a huff. "I'm the official who's going to check into this. Me. In a much more personal way."

"*Jeez*, you're stubborn."

"It's the way to get things done." She pulled herself out of the chair.

Before she could walk away, Elliot caught her in his arms and brought her closely against himself. His eyes seemed to burn into hers. "Please tell me that you've got your head straight about what you're doing."

"It's straight."

"I don't want you getting hurt."

Touched as she was by his concern, she wasn't about to let it restrict her. "I have to do what I have to do," she told him, motivated by all the hurt she already felt.

Sitting at the motel desk that afternoon, Jody got frustratingly involved in the task of trying to track down Susan Windle. Was she still in rehab? Or out? She tried the in-route first, which eventually directed her search to the out-route. Not an easy trail. Anyone she'd found to have information on Susan was very reluctant to give it out. Elliot had been right, she should've just asked Mad first off if she had a phone number for her mother. But from what little Mad seemed to know about her mother, it seemed unlikely that she would. And there was no way Claire, if she did have a number, would've shared it. It was up to Jody to get it on her own.

Finally acquiring Susan's number turned out being the easy part. Dialing it was the hardest. It was scary. And then, prolonging the agony, no one answered on her three different time-spaced calls.

Finally a woman picked up.

"Is this Susan Windle?" Jody nervously asked.

"It is," replied a pleasant voice that Jody nevertheless hated right off.

"My name is Jody Mitchell. I live in Myre, Minnesota. I'm a neighbor to your mother and your daughter."

The line went silent.

"Hello?" Jody had to ask.

"Yeah. What's this about?" The pleasant voice now hardened.

"I'm concerned about Mad."

Silence.

"I was wondering…" Jody carried on, "I mean…after calling every rehab facility in New York I found out, after finding the right one, that you'd been discharged and were on your own now. It…it wasn't easy finding you. And I…I was wondering…hoping… that you might be coming here for a visit some time soon. Like…so we could have a talk or something, you and me?"

It sounded like Susan lit a cigarette.

"She's not sick or hurt or anything like that," Jody said, following the sound of Susan's exhale.

"So what, exactly, is your concern?"

"I don't think your daughter is in the best of care with your mother. I'm not sure if you're aware of it, living so far away, but your mom…she drinks."

"Yes, I know that she has a—"

"A *lot*. And she's neglecting many of Madison's needs, in my opinion."

"Your opinion?"

The Way Forward

"In my opinion, yes. Enough that I felt the need to track you down and let you know."

"But you said Maddy's okay."

"For now, yes, sort of. But the way things are going—"

"Going?"

"I just thought that if you could—"

"You thought?" Susan was making mockery out of Jody's desperation.

It influenced Jody to back off and thus now become the silent one.

After a time Susan asked, "Are you there?"

"Yes," was the most Jody could say.

Following the sound of Susan taking another drag from her cigarette and then slowly exhaling it, she advised her caller, "As for your being concerned for my daughter …*don't be*. I don't much care for budinskys."

"I don't mean to sound like one," Jody tried. "It's just that—"

Click. The line went dead.

There. She'd talked to Mad's mother. Except that she sure wasn't feeling any better for it. She'd failed at getting through to Susan. How disappointing to find that she'd been just as difficult to deal with as Claire. Jody felt her hopefulness fading. She wished now that she hadn't even called Susan Windle. She wished now that…

"Hey!" Don popped into the office unexpectedly.

Elliot came from the back room, smartly greeting him with, "What are you doing here? You no longer work here, remember?"

"Sunday. Day off."

"Of which some of us don't have," Elliot remarked.

Don held a hand over his heart. "Okay, okay…rub it in. Fact is, my heart is still in this motel, and I came over to tell you I'm free to baby sit it if you guys want some getaway time."

"Don't you have a family to spend your Sundays with now?" Jody asked him.

"Yeah, right," he scoffed. "The two of them drove to Duluth for the day. Kenny's never been to Duluth before, except for his plane landing."

"You weren't invited?" Elliot was surprised.

Don hung his head. "We…Nora and me…had a little tiff."

"*Another one?*" Elliot exclaimed.

"What this time?" Jody dared to ask.

"Some guy at the bar last night made a pass at her."

"That pretty much happens to all girls all the time at all bars?" Jody rationed.

"This guy," Don added, "he knows that Nora and I are married."

"So this pass…" Elliot rubbed his chin and weedled his way into the matter like a psychologist, "you're taking that to be Nora's fault?"

"She led him on," Don denoted bitterly. "When he smiled at her she... she winked at him."

"Ah...a smile and a wink," Elliot said dramatically. "Naughty, naughty. If I were you I'd paddle her hide and ground her for a month. And I sure wouldn't have allowed her a trip to Duluth."

Don let out his frustration by slamming the heel of his hand against a wall.

"Hey! Watch it!" Elliot blasted him. "It hasn't been that long since you redid that wall. What is it with you and Jody that you both have the need to hit something or someone?"

"How's Mad?" Don suddenly became aware of other people's problems.

"We picked her up last night and brought her here to sleep," Jody said. "Then I took her back this morning to that awful grandmother of hers."

"Claire's hard to figure all right. It's good you guys stepped in." Rubbing his head and turning in an aimless circle, Don was not yet over his Nora problem. "I didn't like her behaving like she wasn't married. It really pissed me off."

Jody was starting to feel more sorry for her brother's frustrations than her own. She went to give him a sisterly hug. "It's probably going to take a while for you guys to settle into being married. You haven't exactly known each other very long yet."

"Does that give an automatic allowance for her behavior?" Don chided.

"Listen to yourself," Jody blamed him. "Talk to her about it like an adult."

"This coming from *you*?" Elliot cracked.

Jody socked him in the arm.

Clutching his arm dramatically, Elliot turned the conversation. "Hey, Don, I've got a baseball game going on the TV in the back room. How about watching it with me?"

Don liked the idea, smiled and headed for the break room.

"I'm going back to the cottage for a nap," Jody told Elliot wearily.

"Wait," he stopped her. "You did get Susan on the phone, right?"

"You didn't hear me talking to her?"

"Yeah, sort of, I don't know. McConnell hit a homerun and...and then Don came in and—"

"I talked with her."

"So all right. Then that's good, huh?"

Jody moaned.

"So you can tell me about it later, okay?"

Jody said nothing, which Elliot seemed to take as a yes, which therefore seemed to give him permission to return to the baseball game.

Jody left the motel and walked the path to the cottage. Susan was out of the picture now, as far as she was concerned. That left only Claire to deal with. Along with the need of a whole new strategy.

Chapter 12

While Kenny watched a movie on the living room TV Sunday night, Don had Nora to himself, sort of, in the kitchen. They ate ice cream and talked of their day. She'd expressed that she and her son had had a great time in Duluth. And Don expressed that he'd enjoyed watching a baseball game with Elliot.

When Don had had enough small talk, he confessed to Nora, "I missed you like crazy."

"You could've come with us."

"I know."

"I asked you to."

"I know. I'm sorry about not understanding that bar-room thing."

"That's why you wouldn't join Kenny and me?"

"No. Yes. Partly. But mostly I thought you might like some time alone with Kenny since you'd been separated for so long."

She smiled lovingly at him. "Thank you. And…I'm glad you missed me."

They leaned forward, meeting over the table to exchange a kiss.

"About last night…" Don began, settling back on his chair.

"Mark and I," Nora was quick to say, "we're friends, that's all. With a…"

"With what?" Don worried.

"A little casual affection between us."

Don gave an understanding nod without understanding it in the least. He didn't feel better for the term, he felt worse. But he forced himself to give it up and changed the subject. "When Jody and Elliot left Maxy's they picked up Mad and took her to his place for the night. They were really upset that Claire left her granddaughter alone like that. And I sure don't much like the idea of it either."

"Me, neither. I guess there are more sides to people than we normally see. Scary, huh? You know, I've yet to meet this little girl named Mad."

"She's adorable."

"So what do you think of Claire wanting you and me to adopt her? Can you imagine!"

"Life's full of surprises these days, y'know that?" Don took a spoonful of ice cream into his mouth, savoring the taste before it slid down his throat. "First the purchase of the Pinewood Motel, then you happening to me, now Kenny being here, and the latest being the possibility of our taking Mad."

"All of which started back to the time when Jody found you and forced your life back on track, right?" Nora said, knowing the whimsical story of his kidnapping.

He laughed. "You mean, all that I have I owe to Jody?"

"She's a good sister."

"Head strong."

"It obviously runs in the family."

The two of them were laughing as Kenny wandered into the kitchen, his movie interrupted by a string of commercials. "Do I smell ice cream?"

"In the freezer," Nora invited him to help himself.

Don got up to fetch his stepson a bowl and spoon. "So tomorrow you start work at the motel, huh?"

"Yeah. Thanks for the use of your bike so I can get there."

Don studied the boy with a sense of fatherly pride and responsibility. "I want you to know…it's not going to be like this for long?"

Dishing up his ice cream at the counter, Kenny turned his head to look back at him with puzzlement.

"I mean, the three of us living in this little cabin. Your mom and me, we're going to be looking for a house. Not a big fancy house, but bigger and better than this place. And you'll have a room of your own. And—"

"And you might have a little sister," Nora added whimsically.

Kenny's mouth dropped.

"No," she added, "I'm not pregnant. There's this little girl, Mad…"

"Oh, I met her at the motel," Kenny said.

"Did you?" Nora was surprised.

"So what'd you think of her?" Don asked Kenny.

Amidst shoveling a heaping spoonful of ice cream into his mouth, he managed to say, "Amazing kid."

Don explained, "She lives with her grandmother who…who isn't exactly caring for her in the best of ways. And this grandmother, Claire, she'd like Nora and me to adopt Mad."

"Wow!" Kenny exclaimed. "Just like that she can give the kid away?"

"Well, not exactly that easily, but it can be done. She has full custody and legalities could be worked out."

"So what do you think?" Nora asked Kenny.

"Great," was his simple reply, ahead of going back to the TV.

Nora's eyes widened as she grinned at Don. "What can I say…he's easy."

"Just like his ma," Don quipped.

Nora frowned. "Hey…I'm not easy."

"No?" Don took pleasure in teasing her. "If marrying a guy you only know for two weeks isn't easy, I don't know what is."

"Maybe it was the most difficult thing I'd ever done.

Don wasn't sure how to take that.

Nora left her chair and came around the table to sit on his lap. "You had me packing a bag for Vegas so fast I forgot my heels and thus got married in my pink dress and clunky tennis shoes."

Don gave a phony sympathetic moan. "Poor baby…"

"I wanted to buy a new pair of shoes out there, but you wouldn't let me. You thought the combination was cute."

He nodded. "It felt like a sign."

"A sign? I was so embarrassed."

"A sign as to your being my kind of girl…*casual*."

"Crazy," she reinterpreted it.

"Crazy and casual…yep, that's my girl." He kissed her passionately, proving the fixation he had on her character.

"I love being your crazy, casual wife," she murmured.

* * *

At Elliot's place he and Jody also had a movie going on their TV. Though Elliot was somewhat enjoying it, he noticed Jody, beside him on the couch, was dozing off and on and missing much of it. Understanding the trying day she'd had, he could only be glad to see her getting some form of rest. When she'd told him about her not having gotten anywhere with Susan on the phone that afternoon, he'd been emotionally hit and sorry, for he, too, had had his own high hopes about making things right for Mad.

When the next commercial came on, blaring in higher volume, it woke Jody with a startle. She jumped and blinked and found Elliot watching her.

"Hey, sleepyhead," he greeted her.

"Sorry," she apologized groggily.

"For what?"

"I'm not very good company, am I?"

"Hey, you live here now and you're not expected to act like company. You can do whatever you feel like doing without an apology or explanation."

"Really?" she pushed the fact teasingly.

"Well…" he reconsidered.

Pulling herself up from the couch with a moan, she asked, "Got any ice cream?"

Elliot went to the kitchen with her. "Though you may not have officially lived here until now, I think you know that I always have ice cream on hand. He took two bowls out of the cupboard, two spoons and a scooper from a drawer, and dished up two large servings of vanilla ice cream.

When he turned around to give Jody hers, he found her sitting on a chair with her head down on the table. He lifted her head up and stuck her bowl of ice cream before her. Then he picked up her right hand and stuck a spoon into it. "A little tired, are we?"

When he sat down across from her with his ice cream and opened up the jar of chocolate fudge topping, Jody said, "How can you spoil the flavor of vanilla by drowning it with that?"

"I'm a chocoholic, you're a vanillaholic."

"Why don't you just buy chocolate ice cream?"

"Because I know you favor vanilla."

She smiled and started eating.

With a mountain of chocolate added to his vanilla he, too, starting eating. "Good, huh?"

"Good, yeah." She kept the spoonfuls going. "I hated Susan's attitude on the phone this afternoon."

"I know. But then, what did you expect from her, really?"

"Too much."

"Yeah, same here."

"How can a mother be like that about her little girl?"

"I don't know."

Jody gave a weary sigh. "I guess I do know, don't I? I gave away my baby when—"

"Come on, Jody, your situation was entirely different and you know it. Don't compare."

When she closed up, not saying anything after that, Elliot eventually offered, "*Man*, I wish I could help lighten your load."

"The ice cream helps."

He laughed. "I'll pick up a couple more gallons tomorrow."

"Am I *that* bad?"

He studied her seriously. "I wish you'd learn that you can't solve all the problems of the world."

The Way Forward

"I've eased up on Don, haven't I?"

"Yeah, I guess, for now. Only to take on Mad."

"It's like…she's becoming my responsibility."

Elliot threw his left hand into the air "See what I mean."

"You said you wished you could help lighten my load. I'd like that. If you'll just support me on this, that would really help."

"I am. You know I am. If only—"

"If only what?"

"If I knew you weren't relating Mad to your own lost daughter."

"How can I not?" she pleaded, as if her heart were breaking.

"I don't know. But I do know that it's dangerous. You're setting yourself up to get hurt."

"And what's Mad getting set up for?"

"She's got a mother and a grandmother."

"*Does she?*" Jody questioned.

If Elliot were to acknowledge that Jody was right in this debate, he could not do it without a warning. But he knew she was too tired and stressed right now to listen to warnings. It would be better to have this heavy of a talk some other time.

They finished the rest of their ice cream in silence. Then Elliot rinsed the bowls in the sink, suggesting, "It's late, let's forget the rest of the movie, turn off the TV and go to bed."

When he turned around, Jody was giving him a look that rendered his quickly adding, "To bed…in our separate bedrooms…you know that's what I meant."

She nodded, said good night, and headed for her room. Elliot remained standing in the middle of the kitchen for a long while, with the frenzy of a million unsettled thoughts spinning around in his head. Jody did this to him. She'd always done this to him. He should be dizzied out of his mind by now.

Maybe he was.

Maybe he liked it.

Maybe he should just go to his own room and try to sleep it off.

Chapter 13

After a week's time Kenny proved to be working out well as the Pinewood's new part-time employee. Both Jody and Elliot were impressed that he so willingly did what he was told and gave no smart teen-age comebacks. He was a responsible hard worker and a pleasure to be around.

"You're doing a really good job," Jody told him for the umpteenth time as they took a lemonade break in the back yard one afternoon.

"Thanks," he responded appreciatively, sitting on the grass with his back against the oak tree while Jody sat in the tire swing and Mad chased butterflies amidst the flowers. "I'm used to work. I've had to help either my mom or my dad with a lot of stuff since I was a kid. Plus I've had several different paying jobs here and there more recently."

"How long have you been a victim of a broken home?"

Kenny's laugh held a sad slant. "Long as I can remember."

"And you've shifted back and forth between them?"

"There's not going to be anymore shifting. I'm staying with my mom from here on. My mom and Don."

Jody was still finding it hard to believe that her brother had so suddenly become a *stepfather*. "You and Don seem to hit it off well."

"Yeah, I'd say so," Kenny spoke with notable admiration.

"He was so ready to go back to his previous logging job. Once the remodeling work was done around here he did start getting pretty restless."

"Maybe he can get me into logging some day."

"You're saying that *you're* getting restless around here too already?"

Kenny laughed. "No. At least not yet."

"Good. I understand your mom and Don want to find a house."

Kenny nodded. "My mom's never had a real house."

"And your dad?"

"He lives in a cheap mobile home. Really cheap, really old. He could do better for himself, but he doesn't want to. He has no drive or direction in his life. All he cares about is drinking with his low-life friends. That's all. I'd never want to become him."

"Sounds like coming to live with your mom was a good choice."

Kenny lowered his gaze. "My dad…he, uh…was actually glad to see me go."

"I'm sorry."

"Me too. But I'm here now," he stated with a lift in his voice, "and I'm happy that my mom met Don. I guess it was kind of fast, but—"

"*Kind of?*" Jody laughed.

Kenny laughed as well. "Sometimes fast is better than slow. And speaking of fast… their adoption consideration sure came pretty fast."

Jody blinked her eyes with bewilderment. "Adoption?"

"So fast I guess you hadn't heard yet." Kenny motioned to Mad. "My mom and Don are considering the possibility of adopting her."

"Y-you're kidding." Jody felt totally dumbfounded and a little sick to her stomach. She took a sip of lemonade, hoping it would clear her senses, but it didn't.

"You seem really shocked," Kenny observed.

"I am. Yes, I am. How did they—"

"Hey, here's where you guys disappeared to," Elliot came out the back door and toward them, sounding as if he'd been searching for them for hours.

Kenny swiftly got to his feet. "Just taking a break."

Elliot shooed his hand at him. "It's okay, it's okay. Relax."

"I finished that list of things you gave me to do. And I'm ready for more now."

Elliot turned his focus to Jody. "You okay?"

She got out of the swing and handed him the remainder of her lemonade. "Here, you can finish this."

"So…" he grinned with puzzlement as he took it, "would this be a yes or a no?"

Mad came running across the lawn, calling, "Kenny… Kenny…can you take me home to get Nips?"

"Nips?" Jody and Elliot questioned in unison.

"Her stuffed dog," Kenny said, as if he'd now come to know her and her needs better than they did.

Jody and Elliot exchanged surprised looks.

"Would you mind," Kenny asked, "if I run her home to get it?"

Elliot waved the two of them off. "No. Go. Every girl needs her Nips."

It hadn't taken long for Kenny and Mad to connect. They'd fallen into a routine of him giving her a ride down to her place and back whenever she wanted. And she'd sit propped on the crossbar of his bike, like some little princess. Though there was a big age gap between them, it was sweet how a sense of dependence on her part and a sense of guardianship on his bonded them.

"So…" Elliot began to Jody when they were left alone, "when I asked if you were okay I was handed some lemonade. How about a real answer now?"

"It's Don."

"*Jeez*…why didn't I know that?"

"Kenny just told me that he and Nora are thinking about adopting Mad."

Elliot *wouldn't* have known it, as she herself hadn't heard it until now. Thus he was as shocked as she'd been. "You're kidding."

"It seems Claire suggested it to them."

"You're kidding," Elliot said again.

"I know it sounds like a joke, but it's not according to Kenny."

Elliot shook his head, still trying to get his bearings. "That Claire is crazier than we thought, huh?"

"So is Don if he goes for this."

Elliot scratched his head. "Well…hey…you know, maybe it's not such a bad idea."

"You don't understand!" Jody shrieked.

"No…I guess not."

She stuck her hands on her hips. "It was *me* who discovered her, wasn't it?"

Elliot gave her a duh look. "Oh…Jody…come on…"

"Don't tell me to come on, like you think I should know better."

"I think you should know better," he avowed.

She stared at Elliot with disappointment. He wasn't with her on this, which gave her a horrid sense of loss. Didn't he know how much she needed him right now? Didn't he know how much she needed Mad?

"I need a time out," Jody declared in one of her huffs.

"Yeah, I can see that," Elliot merely said to her back as she headed off.

She cut through the office, grabbed her purse, and went out the front door to her car. This was definitely her battle to handle alone.

Luckily she knew the site where Don was currently working, and despite her misty eyes blurring her vision she drove there now. Somehow he always seemed to be an active source amidst most of her problems. Why was that? she agonized. Did he automatically hate her? Did she automatically *cause* him to hate her?

"Hey…" he greeted her, stopping his work in a pleasant reaction to her surprise visit. But as she strode from her car toward him he could see it was more of an attack.

The Way Forward

"It's about Mad," she disclosed her purpose.

"Yeah, I can *see* you're mad," Don poked fun at her seriousness. He wiped the sweat off his brow with his shirtsleeve and took a drink from his water bottle.

"This isn't funny," she snapped.

"Okay." He immediately sobered.

"Mad," she named her battle. "This is about you and Nora wanting to adopt Mad."

"How'd you know about that already?"

"Kenny."

"Ah…I guess parents should be careful discussing things when little ears are nearby. Yeah, it's true, we're thinking about it."

"What are you trying to do, Don? I mean, suddenly you get married. Suddenly you have a stepson living with you. Now suddenly you're adopting a little girl?"

He tilted his head to one side, as if trying to get a better perspective of her intent. "And your point is?"

"You don't understand," Jody moaned.

"Explain it." Don leaned against a tree and crossed his arms.

"You're being arrogant about this!"

"I don't even know what this *is*!"

"I don't like the idea of you and Nora adopting Mad."

"First of all, that's not yet a certainty. And second of all, what's for you to like or not like about it? Why should it affect you so one way or another? Actually, shouldn't you be happy about the possibility of her getting a better home than she has now? Nora and I could give her that. We're going to be looking for a house soon and— "

"You can't do this to me!" Jody shouted.

"Do what? I'm not getting this."

She stuck her hands on her hips. "You are, but you're just being a brat."

"A brat? Nobody's called me that in over thirty years."

The smirk on Don's face riled Jody all the more. "Stop it!"

He lost his smirk along with his temper. He came off the tree and tossed his hands into the air. "Okay, I'll keep asking…*stop what?*"

"I've waited so long for this and now you just—"

"Waited for what?"

"You can't do this to me!" Jody shouted.

One of the other loggers, just then walking by, laughingly coaxed Jody on. "Give'im hell, little lady! He probably deserves it."

Don gave him the finger. Then continued to Jody, "I don't see as I'm doing anything to you. You're saying a lot of stuff here without really saying anything at all."

"You don't understand," Jody told him again.

"You're right! So if you're not going to say something that says something, I've got work to do." He picked up his chain saw.

Jody headed back to her car, muttering loud enough for him to hear, "You're so dumb you can't see the forest for the trees."

"Cute!" he shouted after her. "Thanks for stopping by. Come again when you can talk like an adult!"

Jody took off with her tires shrieking. *I can't lose her again*, she thought to herself as a mental rerun played in her head of the hospital scene where she handed over her newborn baby girl to a cold-faced nurse.

Chapter 14

They were on their way. To Duluth. The two of them.

"I'm glad your grandma let you go with me," Jody said, taking her eyes off of her driving to smile across at Mad.

Buckled and happy in the passenger seat, Mad giggled. "Me too."

Following her episode with Don, Jody knew what she had to do. She'd gone to the cottage, hurriedly packed some things into a bag without Elliot's knowing, then drove Mad home and had a talk with Claire.

"A little getaway for us," she'd explained to Claire of her request to take Mad along. "I need to pick up some motel supplies, and it would add some fun to it if she could ride with me."

Claire had given her permission easily, almost too easily, and now Jody and Mad were on their way. As far as Elliot knew, they were only going to Duluth to purchase motel needs. He did remark that it was rather late in the day for such a trip, but Jody convinced him that the timing was okay.

"Do you like to drive?" Mad asked, watching her diligently.

Jody'd never given much thought to it until now. "Yeah, I guess I do."

"I'm gonna drive someday. And then I'm gonna go on a long, long trip."

Jody gave her another brief look. "Kind of like this one?"

"Longer."

Jody felt a twinge of guilt for not having told the child that this trip was actually intended to be long. She hadn't told Elliot or Claire the truth of it either. It was a secret that only she herself knew about so far. A secret that made her deliriously happy inside, deep beyond the guilt. This trip was about her spending some quality alone time with her daughter...or uh, *with Mad, the likeness of her daughter.* She needed that more than anything in the whole world right now and she was proud of herself for making it happen.

She glanced at Mad. "So this long, long trip you plan to take some day, does that mean you don't like living with your grandma?"

Mad didn't answer. But her not answering seemed to *be* her answer.

"How would you feel, Mad, about our making this Duluth trip into more than just a one day thing and rather into a long, long trip?"

The girl's attention sharpened. "Really?"

"We could stay for as many days and nights as we wanted. We could make a fun-filled adventure out of this. If you'd like."

"Could we?" Mad exclaimed in the manner of a yes.

Jody laughed. "We can."

"We can let Grandma know."

"Sure."

"And Elliot?"

Jody's answer came slowly. "Sure."

"What about clothes?"

"I have some with me, and we can pick up some for you. Do you like shopping?"

"Yes."

"We'll need toothbrushes and toothpaste and a few things like that. And junk food. Do you like junk food?"

Mad clapped her hands. "Yes! Doritos."

"Are you related to Elliot?" Jody teased her.

Mad didn't get it.

"He loves Doritos, too."

"Yeah…" Mad laughed, "maybe we *are* related."

The drive was pleasant. An overcast sky made it easy on the eyes. Jody turned on the car radio and let Mad find a station she liked.

"I wish they'd play *You Are My Sunshine*."

"That's a pretty old song," Jody said. "I don't imagine it comes up on the radio very often."

"It's a good song."

"It is," Jody agreed.

"It's my favorite."

"I know."

"My mom taught it to me when I was little."

Jody hadn't known that, but knowing it now made her jealous.

When they got to Duluth, Jody drove right past the warehouse where the Pinewood had an account with a discount. She'd lied about needing to purchase motel supplies. If Elliot opened the main supply cupboard at the motel he'd see that it was full and know that she'd only made up this errand as a getaway excuse. She hoped he wouldn't look. At least not yet.

While Mad was totally unmindful that they weren't stopping for supplies, she was totally in tune of the idea of stopping at a McDonalds for lunch. And after that they went next door to the drug store to buy a few things.

"So where will we sleep tonight if we're staying over?" Mad asked.

"I know of a place," Jody said. "I...I was there once with a friend. It's a nice place and not too expensive."

"Is it as nice as the Pinewood?"

"No way. Nothing is. But it's nice."

*   *   *

Before Kenny left the Pinewood for the day, he asked Elliot where Jody had disappeared to.

"Toilet paper, Kleenex and Pinesol," Elliot answered. "And she took Mad along for the ride."

A puzzled look came over Kenny's face.

Elliot further explained, "It would cost way too much to purchase those things, in the quantity we need, here in Myre."

Kenny seemed none the less clear. "It's just that I earlier noticed that the supply cupboard is full. It couldn't be any fuller."

"Oh, yeah?" Elliot marched off to the back room and whipped open a cupboard door. And then another cupboard door. And another. "Damn!"

Kenny stood behind him. "I don't get it."

"I do." Elliot stamped his foot. "Damn!"

"So what's it mean?" Kenny asked.

"I think it means your Aunt Jody flipped out."

"Huh?"

"When you get home," Elliot told him, "have Don call me as soon as he gets there."

"Sure. But about Jody..."

Elliot moaned. "Oh, you've got so much to learn about your Aunt Jody."

When Don called later, all Elliot said to him was, "Get over here ASAP. We need to talk."

Without questioning it, Don said he was on his way. When he got to the motel, Benjamin was there for the night shift and Elliot was waiting outside.

"So what's up?" Don asked, leaving his car and walking toward him. He spoke casually, but looked worried.

"She left with Mad."

"Jody?"

"Of course Jody," Elliot snapped.

"She left with Mad?"

"She took Mad with her to Duluth to pick up supplies." To Don's duh look, he added, "Our supply cupboards are full."

"That's strange."

"Your sister," Elliot bluntly reminded him.

"Yeah," Don acknowledged regrettably. "So what are you thinking?"

"Come on…don't tell me you haven't gotten it by now how Jody relates her own lost daughter to Mad. She thinks Mad is God's replacement gift to her. I think she's just kidnapped the kid."

"No, she wouldn't do that."

"Your sister!"

"Yeah."

"This is your fault, y'know."

Don's gaze narrowed on Elliot. "My fault?"

"It's freaked Jody out, the possibility of you and Nora adopting Mad."

Don ran a nervous hand through his hair. "Yeah…she was trying to tell me as much this afternoon. She came by my site and—"

"You had a clue to this and you didn't do anything?"

"I didn't realize it could be a clue to something like this happening until now. Let's not call it a kidnapping, okay? I mean…how long have they been gone?"

Elliot shrugged. "Three or four hours."

"Well, how about we give them some time before we label this too harshly?"

"Time might be our enemy."

"So what else can we do?"

Elliot shrugged. Having no plan made him feel horribly helpless.

Don quickly seemed to come to the same feeling, and the two of them stood in a long, frustrated silence.

Finally Don decided, "I'm going back home. Call me if you hear anything or think of anything we can do. Okay?"

Elliot gave a nod. Don gave him a pat on the back and left.

Elliot went inside the motel office to say good night to Benjamin. He didn't bother telling him about Jody at this point.

Walking the path to his cottage, Elliot spoke aloud to Jody as if she were walking beside him. "Come on, Jody, wake up. Mad isn't your daughter. She's not. Please get your head straight about this and come back. Please come back, you crazy girl."

He loved her. Times like this, when she drove him to his wit's end, he knew that love could be the only reason he'd endured them. Nevertheless,

The Way Forward

whenever the concept concurred to him it always managed to newly surprise him. Like who would've ever thought he'd get zapped by a crazy, high-strung girl fourteen years his junior? *Jeez.* Did she know the effect she had on him? Maybe. Probably. Did it matter that Jody was going to be Jody, no matter what? Maybe not. Probably not. It only mattered to Elliot that somehow he had to ride the waves with her.

* * *

"It's a nice place," Mad judged their room at the Skyline Motel in Duluth that evening. "But you're right, it's not as nice as the Pinewood."

Jody threw her bag on one of the twin beds and gave a happy sigh of relief to their having arrived. It'd been a pleasant, but long, drive, and her head was feeling crowded. Mad also looked a bit drained.

"There's a restaurant nearby where we can have supper after we rest a while. Why don't you stretch out and take a little nap. Then later, after we eat, maybe we can find a movie to go to if we're feeling refreshed. How's that?"

Mad's smile indicated an overwhelming big yes. Then she yawned and curled up on the bed that was to be hers. Jody tugged a cover loose and pulled it up over the girl. Then she stepped back, holding a warm gaze upon her for a few minutes.

Eventually she sat down on the edge of the other bed and from there observed the room with interest. It wasn't the same room that she and Elliot had shared last summer when they'd stopped for an overnight there amidst their search for Don. But it was in fact the same motel, and it brought a flood of memories back to her.

She'd thought nothing of it, sharing a motel room with her employer-friend at that time. How strange was that? But they'd been tired. Had little money. Needed to rest. Had shared a room with separate beds. Her main focus had been on finding her long lost brother, not about shacking up.

Now, as she thought back to that time, her mixed emotions made her realize how easily something might have happened between her and Elliot. It didn't, but it could have. For even back then there was, as there was now, an unspoken sort of *something* between them. Something that made them close to one another but reluctant to give way to.

Jody dropped back onto her pillow and closed her eyes. Thoughts…so many thoughts spun in her head. It was a dizzy, uncontrollable sensation. A likeness, she supposed, to having downed three vodka-sours fast. Although she'd never drank that recklessly, she'd never been in this reckless of a situation before either.

Well, yes…she had, of course she had. She'd had a baby out of wedlock. In fact, out of actually even caring about the so-called father of her baby. *Spinning, spinning…* her mind was going full speed and nonstop. And as for fathers, they were supposed to know best, weren't they? Well, hers hadn't. He'd pressured her into giving her baby away. She'd only been sixteen, but she could've been a good mother, given the chance.

She should have fought for her baby, but she'd been so passive. *No, Dad, no! Well, okay, Dad, if I have to. But it hurts so bad. God, it just hurts so bad.*

Her own little girl, at this time, would be Mad's age. And she would no doubt look a lot like Mad. *Spinning, spinning…* Jody's mind kept telling her that the girls, they were one in the same. *Wrong…right…possibly…maybe.*

She turned her head and opened her eyes to look across at Mad, who was now sound asleep like a little angel. Jody stared at her until she began to feel a settling sense of peacefulness and acceptance to the here and now. It was like a sleepy, dreamy, mother-daughter sort of contentment.

* * *

"Come on, loosen up…" Nora encouraged Don while massaging his back.

He lay on his stomach in bed, unable to sleep. It helped that Nora stayed awake with him, rubbing his back, speaking to him gently.

"She'll come back tomorrow and everything will be all right," Nora assured him, as if she truly believed it herself.

"You don't know Jody," he stressed. "She's got this stubborn streak. She's got this obsession about the baby she gave away seven years ago. She came to me today, expressing a desperation that I was too bull-headed to get at the time. It scares me that she really might have flipped out. I'm really worried about her, Nora."

"Is there anything we can do?"

"I wish."

"Me too."

Don rolled over, facing his wife, giving her an appreciative look. "Thanks."

She smiled. "You're welcome."

He put his arms around her and pulled her down against him. He kissed her, as if he wasn't quite so worried about his sister now. Nora could turn the whole world around for him when she worked her wonders on him. It seemed like a good time for him to work some wonders on her.

"Hey, Don—" Kenny's voice called from the bottom of the loft ladder.

"*Shit*," Don moaned at the interruption. Then answered his stepson, "Yeah?"

The Way Forward

"The TV remote quit working. Got any batteries?"

Don started to lift himself up from the bed. "I'm not sure. I'll—"

Nora pushed him back down as she called to her son, "Use the buttons on the TV."

Don relaxed at the surprise of more of her wonders. "You're so smart."

"I just didn't want you to leave me right at this moment."

He wrapped his arms around her again. "Smart. Beautiful. Sexy. Heavenly backrubs. Man…have I got a good deal here, or not?"

"So…" she cooed, "you're starting to feel better?"

"There's nobody else in my life right now," he whispered to her. "No Jody, no Elliot, no Kenny. Just you, baby…just you."

Chapter 15

Elliot felt miserable and lonely and worried, getting up the next morning without Jody being at the cottage. Her having stayed there for a time now definitely made her a regular resident. And their sharing a house together had definitely turned their relationship into something more than it'd been before. Exactly what, he wasn't sure. Except that he'd become nicely used to it.

How could she run off with Mad like that? How could she be so irresponsible?

And, God forbid, what if this was something worse? What if they'd been in a car accident? Or abducted by some maniac? And maybe the very worst of all was the pitiful fact that there was nothing he could do but sit and wait.

When the phone rang, he grabbed it on the first ring. "Yeah!"

"Anything?" Don asked.

"No. I was hoping this was Jody."

"It's early. Let's hope she'll call yet this morning."

"We can hope."

Don moaned. "There's gotta be something we can do."

"There is."

"What?"

"I haven't thought of it yet."

"Thanks."

"Don't thank me yet, *not just yet*."

When they hung up, Elliot made some coffee and sat down at his kitchen table. "Oh, Jody...*jeez*, what have you done?"

When the phone rang again, he thought surely it was her.

But it was Claire. "What's she done with my granddaughter?"

Elliot rubbed his head...*like he needed Claire right now*. Yet he really did owe her some equal consideration. "They went to Duluth for supplies," he lied to her for lack of anything more constructive to say at the moment.

"Well, yes, that's what Jody told me," Claire said, none-the less soothed. "But how the hell long does that take anyway?"

"A little longer than usual this time."

"It's the next day, Mr. Smartass!"

"Don't worry, Claire."

"I'm worried!" she shouted. "I'm a good grandmother, for cryin' out loud. Why wouldn't I worry when Mad doesn't come home over night?"

"Yeah, I know," Elliot gave her, though he couldn't get past the fact that she didn't seem to worry that much about the kid's welfare before now. "I'm checking on things, okay? It'll be all right. Mad's in good hands. I'll get back to you when I know something."

Claire slammed her phone down without a thank you or good-bye.

Elliot sank back down onto a kitchen chair. *Man*, the things Jody put him through. The kidnapping of her own brother last year. And now, it seemed, the kidnapping of Mad. He'd been in on the brother one with her, but not this one. If he had been, it surely wouldn't have even happened. At least he didn't think it would. And yet… Jody could be so persuasive. She could turn him into such a spineless fool.

All of a sudden it came to him, something to try. He called Don. "Get over here. I've got a plan."

"Really?" Don responded excitedly.

"No, I'm lying."

"You do really have a plan?"

"There's a slight chance that Jody and Mad might be staying at the Skyline Motel in Duluth."

"And where's this out-of-the-blue idea coming from?"

"Past experience."

"Huh?"

"When Jody and I were on our journey to find you last year, we spent a night there, at the Skyline."

"You and my sister—"

"Not like you think. But if she and Mad went to Duluth, and it got late and they needed a place to stay, a *cheap* place, Jody might have gone back there out of her familiarity with it."

Don moaned.

"Thanks for your confidence," Elliot scowled. "So this might only be a slight chance, but it's better than none, right?"

Don sighed. "I know. You're right. Sorry. I was just hoping for something much more."

"I know. Me, too. Anyway, we gotta go check it out."

"I'm due at work in half an hour."

"Screw work. If missing a day cost you your job you can always come back here and work. Give your sister and Mad some priority right now. Come on! Time's wastin'! We gotta find Jody and Mad before Claire, bless her sweet heart, gets the police involved in this."

"She'd do that?" Don gasped.

"You might think so if you'd heard her on the phone like I did a while ago."

"See you in ten," Don said, hanging up.

While Elliot waited for him, he called information to obtain the phone number for Duluth's Skyline Motel. He wished he'd have thought of doing this in the first place.

In another couple of minutes, he was responding to the desk clerk's inability to help him. "You're sure? No one's registered under Jody Mitchell? *Jody Mitchell.*"

"Sorry, sir."

"Look again," Elliot pleaded.

After a pause the response was the same, "Sorry, sir."

Elliot hung up in a new wave of disappointment. And yet, of course, if Jody were trying to escape, and wanted to make sure she couldn't be found, she probably wouldn't have used her real name at the Skyline. Nevertheless... it would still be worth it for him and Don to go there in person. If necessary they'd raid every room themselves. Elliot wished he had ten more backup ideas toward finding her, but so far this was the only one.

He hurried down the path to the Pinewood to ask Benjamin if he could work the entire day and possibly more. Good 'ol Benjamin was willing and asked no questions, but Elliot briefly told him the story. Then he stepped outside and waited for Don in the parking lot.

When Don arrived he had Kenny with him and the bike in the trunk. Though the boy surely wouldn't be expected to handle the office on his own for a day yet, he would be of assistance to Benjamin.

"Let's go," Elliot said, jumping into Don's car beside him.

"Did you bring the handcuffs?" Don joked as they drove off.

"I think we can handle her single-handedly."

Don laughed. "Let's hope."

* * *

The Way Forward

"How about this one?" Jody asked, holding up a bright, multi-colored tee-shirt to Mad."

"I love it!" she replied, clutching one that she herself had also chosen off the display table, a blue one with a robin on the front.

"How about both of them?" Jody said, more as a decision than a question.

They added both shirts to the cart, which also held two pair of shorts, a pair of jeans, and some socks and underwear for Mad, plus a few big-girl things for Jody.

Mad was more excited than Jody'd ever seen her. "I haven't had new clothes in like forever. Thank you, Jody. I love this stuff!"

"Good. Anyway, they're a necessity for our trip."

"We could've packed stuff at home before we left."

Jody tapped her forehead, as if she'd stupidly overlooked the idea. "I know. What was I thinking? Or not thinking? Anyway, shopping for new stuff is more fun, right?"

"Right," the girl giggled. "I like the stuff you bought for you, too."

"We're going to be the best-dressed chicks in town," Jody exclaimed, pushing their cart to the checkout counter.

They'd been in the department store since it first opened at nine o'clock. And now, with their shopping finished, they were going to go somewhere for breakfast. It was going to be a wonderful day.

It was great having Mad at her side. It was great hearing her react so happily to the slightest little things. Jody loved making her happy. And Mad probably had no idea whatsoever how very happy she was making Jody. The rest of the world seemed gone, at least from any of their concern. It was just the two of them in a world of their own.

"What are we going to do the rest of the day?" Mad asked later when they'd finished their breakfast in a quaint little restaurant.

"We're going to have fun," Jody said. Though right off she had absolutely no idea what that might involve, she did know for certain that almost anything would work.

"I like having fun with you," Mad said, taking Jody's hand as they left the restaurant and walked to the car.

Jody felt tears welling in her eyes. She blinked them back and smiled down at her daughter. *No, not daughter...* her daughter-like little friend. She knew that and was okay with it. She was truly enjoying this for what it was.

"Maybe we could go to another movie," Mad suggested. "Grandma never took me to any."

"Maybe we could go to *two* of them," Jody said. "One before lunch and one after lunch."

"And one more tonight?" Mad pushed it with a giggle.

"Maybe," Jody said, giggling girlishly herself.

Chapter 16

"This is it?" Don asked, pulling into the lot Elliot had directed him to.

"Skyline Motel," Elliot verified. He was unbuckled and starting to open his door before Don completely brought the car to a stop.

"Good luck to us," Don said hopefully, removing his key from the ignition. He got out and joined Elliot on the walk to the office.

Elliot's knees felt quivery and the palms of his hands sweaty. This was a long shot, hoping to find Jody and Mad here. But if they weren't here, he had no other idea.

"You okay?" Don asked him.

"No. You?"

"No. I'm not seeing her car in the lot."

"Me neither. But that doesn't necessarily mean she's not here."

The two of them burst into the motel office something like a couple of outlaw bank robbers. The man working at the counter flinched in astonishment and offered no greeting.

"Jody Mitchell," Elliot said. "We'd like to know if she's here."

Skeptical of the request, the desk clerk nevertheless checked the computer. "Sorry… no one by that name is registered."

"Lemme look," Elliot said.

The clerk held up a stop hand to him. "I'm afraid not, sir. You asked for a name and I told you it's not here. That's it."

Elliot leaned an elbow on the counter. "Y'know…I run a motel in Myre and—"

"Where?" the clerk asked.

The Way Forward

Elliot rolled his eyes and chuckled, despite his frustration. "Everybody always asks that. It's a lot farther north than Duluth. It's...*up there*. Anyway, at my motel we try to accommodate people's—"

"This is the big city. Harsh as it may seem, we don't accommodate people beyond renting them rooms. Sorry."

"I stayed here once myself," Elliot stated, hoping to influence him.

It didn't work. The clerk's face clearly read *case closed*.

"Let's go," Don said, tugging Elliot's arm.

The guys went outside, but did not immediately get into Don's car. They stood in the parking lot, gazing back at the long, two-story building.

"She's here," Elliot insisted. "I know it. I can feel it."

"Well, if she is," Don said, "she's not now, and she's registered under another name."

"I might've found her if that jerk would've let me at the computer. Her bogus name might've somehow just jumped out at me."

"Yeah, right," Don doubted it. "So now what?"

"We wait. We sit in your car and wait. Until she comes back."

"A stakeout," Don ridiculed the idea.

"Got a better idea?"

"No."

"There's a restaurant near by. Let's go pick up some donuts and coffee and come back here to sit it out."

As they got into the car, Don quipped, "You sure like to play P.I., don't you?"

"And I'm good, huh?"

Don laughed. "Right down to the coffee and donuts."

*   *   *

Jody and Mad left the movie theater late that afternoon and went to McDonald's for supper. Though Mad hadn't been to many McDonald's in her young and sheltered life she was now claiming it as her favorite restaurant.

"I can't believe how little you've seen of McDonald's and movie theaters," Jody remarked to her as they ate. "It seems that at home with your grandma you're allowed way too much freedom, while in the outer world you've barely been anywhere."

Mad dragged a French fry through a puddle of ketchup. "If I had a mother...I could go a lot of places."

Tenderly assuming that position, Jody said, "We can go to a lot of places together, you and me."

"What about Elliot?" Mad suddenly seemed to come aware of what they'd left behind.

"What about him?" Jody played innocent.

"Isn't he going to worry about us being gone like this?"

"I called him last night after you'd fallen asleep," she said. Then immediately sorry for lying, she tried making up for it with a closer actuality. "He's usually okay with my decisions."

Mad smiled cutely and let it go at that. "I like being with you, Jody. We have fun together, don't we?"

It was music to Jody's ears. She sipped her vanilla shake through a straw, managing to smile back at Mad at the same time. Fun was such a small word to fit the magic that'd come into her world. Who would've thought that something like this would ever happen? That suddenly this wonderful little girl would come into her life to fill the void of her having lost her own little girl years ago?

"What're we gonna do next?" Mad asked.

"I think we'll go down to the shore of Superior and throw rocks into the water."

"It's a really big lake, isn't it?" Mad exclaimed, recollecting her amazement of having seen it for the very first time yesterday.

"It's huge. And beautiful. I picked up a disposable camera in the drug store earlier so we can take pictures."

"My grandma has only one picture of me," Mad said sadly, "It's of when I was a baby. I think five months old."

"Your grandma…" Jody began slowly and carefully, "she has problems, doesn't she? Not just with you, honey, but with her own self. I think you need to know that and be understanding of that."

The girl nodded. She was a smart kid and surely already knew that something wasn't right with Claire.

"Let's go," Jody said when they'd finished eating.

"Yeah," Mad cheered, bounding out of the booth, "let's go."

*   *   *

When Don dozed off from sitting too long in the warm, sun-grazed car, Elliot bumped his arm and brought him back.

"W-what…?" he asked groggily.

"Your watch. My turn to nap."

"Some more of your cop talk?" Don asked bitterly.

"We've come this far, we can't afford to miss her when she comes back here."

Don straightened up in his seat and looked through the windshield at the parking lot. "Like it's a sure thing that Jody and Mad are staying here.

The Way Forward

Come on, Elliot, I'm as determined as you are to find them, but maybe we're just wasting time sitting here and should be—"

"What?" Elliot snarled. "Running all over Duluth on a wild goose chase? This is our best chance. I think maybe our *only* chance." He paused to rub his aching head. "*Jeez*, Don…I sure don't know what else to do."

"I'm hungry. We didn't have lunch and it's already supper time," Don complained.

"You ate a half dozen donuts," Elliot reminded him.

"Hardly a hamburger steak."

"I need a nap. Your watch."

"You're gonna let me starve?"

"Yes."

"Thanks. Okay…go ahead and take your nap."

"You'll watch?" Elliot verified

"Yeah."

As Elliot slid down in his seat and closed his eyes, he mumbled to Don, "Don't miss anything."

Chapter 17

Elliot woke up from his nap, surprised to find it had grown dark out. He straightened up in his seat, looked to his left, and found Don slouched down behind the steering wheel *asleep*.

"Wake up!" Elliot shouted at him. "Wake up!"

Don moved some, opened his eyes, and squinted at Elliot. "*What?*"

"You're shift! This was supposed to be your shift and you fell asleep."

Yawning and looking out the windows, Don, too, was surprised at the darkness. "What the hell time is it?"

"It doesn't matter. Except that it was *your* time to watch and you blew it."

"Yeah, well, I got drowsy just sitting here and I guess I dozed off."

Elliot mumbled a few cuss words under his breath, then snarled at Don, "We could've missed Jody and—"

"Wait!" Don pointed to the entrance end of the parking lot. "There's her car."

"I'll be damned!" Elliot exclaimed. "I was right. She's staying here. She must've drove in while we were both sleeping."

The guys got out of Don's car and hurried toward the motel office.

"We still don't know what room she's in," Don said.

"Let me handle this, okay?" Elliot advised him.

The same clerk was behind the desk, immediately recognizing the guys as they burst through the door.

"There's this car out in the lot—" Elliot excitedly began.

"Ah, yes..." the clerk nodded, "precisely where a car ought to be."

"It's lights were left on. It belongs to this person we're looking for, and if I give you the license plate number you could—"

The Way Forward

Holding up a stop hand to Elliot, the clerk left his station and went to take a look out the big front window that overlooked the entire parking lot. Then he returned to the counter, shaking his head and asserting, "There are no car lights on out there."

Elliot gave an impatient sigh. "She's here...this Jody girl...now are you—"

"I told you, there's no Jody registered."

"I know. But see...she must've checked in under a different name. *Jeez*, don't you ask for I.D.s here?"

"I have nothing more to tell you."

"Oh, I think you've got a lot more to tell us," Elliot insisted.

"I think not."

"If we could just take a look on your computer," Don suggested, "we could probably figure out what name she—"

"I'm going to have to ask the two of you leave."

"We're not criminals," Elliot stressed, his voice rising. "This guy here is her brother. And I'm—"

"He's Elliot." Don filled in. "A friend. A good friend of hers and mine."

The clerk pointed to the door. "I've had enough of you two. Either you go or I'll call the police."

Elliot tightened his mouth and balled his fists. As he took a step forward, Don stopped him from behind, saying, "Let's go."

Not yet ready to leave, Elliot begged the clerk further. "She's about five- six... dark hair...early twenties...cute as a button...and she has a little seven-year old girl with her, also cute as a button. How many of your guests fit that description? Now...if you won't co-operate in helping us find this missing two-some, *I'll* call the police. Nice newspaper article, wouldn't you say? Duluth's Skyline Motel refuses to bend rules in time of emergency."

The clerk looked back and forth between Don and Elliot. "You didn't say this was an emergency."

Elliot gave a huff, frustrated that his desperation hadn't revealed as much.

The clerk expressed his own frustration. "How do I know where you're really coming from?"

"I already told you...*Myre*."

"I mean your purpose. What kind of emergency."

Elliot gave another impatient huff. "Aren't you listening? This girl... Jody. That's all you need to know. The police can fill you in on the rest if I get them out here. Okay if I use your phone?"

"Sir," the clerk persisted nervously, "you don't understand. I have responsibilities here, and I can't afford any trouble."

Elliot leaned across the counter and grabbed a handful of the man's shirt. "Then I suggest you tell us what we need to know."

The clerk looked at Don, and Don gave a nod that reinforced Elliot's threat. Pressured into it, he told the guys, "I'm not liking this…room 27, second floor."

Elliot opened his hand.

"No key. That's as far as I go. You knock on her door and it's up to her if you go in or not."

"Fair," Don said, giving Elliot a shove toward the stairs.

"You'd think a swanky place like this would have an elevator, wouldn't you?" Elliot wisecracked on their way up.

"Shut up," Don advised him.

* * *

Jody was astounded at the knock on the door.

"Who's that?" Mad asked, sitting on her bed looking at a comic book.

"I'll find out." Jody looked through the door's peephole. "What are *you* guys doing here?" she exclaimed, shocked at the sight of Elliot and Don.

"Better question," Don retorted, "what are *you* doing here?"

"Open the door, Jody," Elliot said.

She opened it and the guys entered. She closed the door behind them and stuck her hands on her hips. "What is this? What's going on?"

"Exact same questions we have for you," her brother said.

"Did you come to join our holiday?" Mad asked Elliot and Don.

"Holiday?" Don answered her question with his question, then gave Jody a narrowed look.

"That's what you're calling this?" Elliot asked Jody. "A holiday?"

Before she could answer yes or no, which she had no intention of doing anyway, he added, "Because I can think of a better name for it."

Mad put her comic book aside and stared at the guys in puzzlement.

"Speaking of names," Don said to Jody, "what one did you use when you registered here?"

"What do you mean?"

"Jody Mitchell wasn't in the computer," Elliot told her.

"So how did you find me?"

"Physical description."

Jody rolled her eyes.

"Are we lost?" Mad asked, starting to be scared.

"No," Jody told her. Then she told Elliot and Don, "You guys are intruding. You have no reason to be here. Mad and I…we're fine."

The Way Forward

"Define fine," Elliot challenged her. He gave a quick glance over at Mad, then spoke lower and more personally to Jody. "We were worried about you. You've done a really dumb thing here. Maybe you should just try explaining it now if you can."

Don agreed. "Yeah, let's hear your story, Jody."

Jody's concern was on Mad, her sitting there watching and listening and taking all this in but not understanding it. "This isn't the time," she told the guys.

"It's exactly the time," Elliot held his ground with her. "Don, why don't you stay with Mad…look at comics with her…while Jody and I step outside and talk."

Jody didn't want to go. She didn't want to talk. She didn't want to bring her special time with Mad to a halt. But neither did she want to make this into any more of a scene in front of the child than it had already been. With a shove from Elliot, she told Mad she'd be right back, then she left with him.

As they reached the bottom of the stairs and started across the lobby toward the front door, the desk clerk asked, "Is everything all right, Miss Hasslehoff?"

"No," Jody grunted.

"Hasslehoff?" Elliot snickered. Then tightening his grasp on her arm, he advised her, "Tell him it is or he'll have the cops here in a matter of minutes."

Jody gave the desk clerk a forced smile and changed her tune. "I'm kidding, everything's fine."

"Fine," he said, as if the word burned his tongue.

When they got outside, Jody burst with questions to Elliot. "What's that about? What's wrong with the desk guy? Why did he look at us like that?"

"Long story. Skip it. Let's get to yours."

"I have no story. I just…I had this need to spend some alone time with Mad. Maybe I didn't handle it so well, but—"

"I guess not! Saying that you were going for supplies? When the supply cupboards were full? Without telling anyone that you just might stay in Duluth overnight? Or over summer? Or for whatever you—"

"Nobody would've understood."

She hated the look Elliot was giving her as he said, "So you thought it might be easier for everyone to understand kidnapping?"

"Kidnapping?" she gasped. "Where do you get that?"

"You take a child away from her home and extend your so-called holiday together on the sneak…that's kidnapping."

She stuck her hands on her hips. "I don't see it that way."

Elliot shook his head and sighed. "Jody, Jody...what way, in heaven's name, *do* you see it? No, never mind. I know. Of course, I know. You like thinking that Mad's your daughter, don't you?"

"I know she's not mine, but she's *like* mine. How can I not see that, think that? You don't know how special Mad is to me."

"Oh, but I do know. You don't think that I haven't ached right along with you over this? You don't think that my knowing you as long as I have hasn't enabled me to read you like a book? Well...except for one missing page. The page that gives you permission to take Mad off like this? *Jeez*, I wish I had that page. Because though I think I've truly been in tune with your feelings over your lost baby, and your heartfelt connection to Mad, and the hundred and one other things you get so wrapped up over, your running off with Mad just doesn't compute with me. You've really lost me there, Jody. And I'm scared to think that maybe you've kind of lost a part of yourself."

Elliot's speech cut deep. It drove Jody to shame and guilt. She tried fighting it despite her weakening resolve. "Maybe I don't have much time. Maybe Don and Nora will be getting Mad soon. Why is Claire giving her to them? I'm more like Mad's mother than Nora ever will be. I know Mad's not mine but I want her to be. I want that so bad."

"Tell me something," Elliot said, looking at her as though he were searching her heart by way of her eyes, "were you even planning to come back at all? Or were you intending to just disappear into the vast universe with Mad?"

"I don't know. I'm not sure." Tears that had been threatening in Jody's eyes now started trickling down her cheeks. "I feel...I just feel this strong responsibility to Mad. And I... like... put that above trying to justify it. I don't *want* to reason it out. I'm afraid to."

"Sometimes facing the right thing to do is pretty scary."

A chill came over Jody, making her quiver. She wasn't sure if it was from the coolness of the evening or the ache of her conscience.

"Let's sit down," Elliot suggested, motioning to the bench at the end of the sidewalk.

"I'm not feeling so good," Jody said as they sat together.

"I know," Elliot sympathized, putting his arm around her shoulder.

She gave him a close look. The neon motel sign shed enough light their way for her to see what she was looking for. The genuineness of this guy was lit up on him as if he were his own personal neon sign. "You *do* know, don't you."

He nodded, saying sadly, "The only thing I don't know is how to make it better for you. How do I do that, huh?"

"Maybe it's not up to you. Maybe it's only up to me."

The Way Forward

"It's just that I feel this strong responsibility," he moaned, playfully mocking her, "and nobody understands and—"

Jody punched him.

"That's my girl," he laughed. "Feeling a little better now, are we?"

A burst of laughter helplessly escaped her. It was a good release. And yes, she was feeling a little better. "I guess you do know how to help me."

"I can make you laugh, yeah…but about the serious stuff…about Mad…"

Jody and Elliot's attention flicked across the parking lot as two squad cars, lights flashing but no sirens, came fast off the street, fast across the lot and screeched to a stop before them. Four police officers jumped out of the cars and rushed forth in the flood of headlights, hands on their holstered guns.

"Don't move!" one of them commanded.

Jody wasn't sure she could move if she wanted to. She felt utterly frozen to the bench.

"*Damn*," Elliot scowled under his breath, "he did it anyway."

"Who? What?" she asked in a sick quiver.

An officer was quicker than Elliot to explain. "Got got a call from the desk clerk."

"No kidding," Elliot snarled.

"He thought we should check this out."

"Check what out?" Jody asked.

"Do you know this guy?" the officer asked.

"What guy?"

"The one you're sitting with. The desk clerk said there was something suspicious going on. Something about this guy arrogantly insisting on getting your room number, then dragging you downstairs and outside."

Jody and Elliot exchanged looks. She resented that Elliot seemed to know what was going on more than she did.

Except for his questioning, "*Dragging?*"

"I'd like to see your I.D., please," an officer told him.

"There must be a terrible misunderstanding here," Jody said defensively, though to what she had no idea. "This is Elliot Treggor. He's my friend. I am not in danger of him. He's done nothing wrong." She paused to give Elliot another look. "*Have you?*"

"I appreciate you're vouching for him, Miss, but it's routine that we check him out."

Elliot handed over his driver's license, and one of the officers took it back to a squad car to run it through the computer.

"What have you done?" Jody whispered to Elliot.

"I wasn't *dragging* you, was I?" he asked her to at least attest to that much.

She looked at the three cops and shook her head. "He was pulling me, only pulling me."

"Thanks," Elliot moaned.

When Jody and Elliot eventually returned to her room, Don, with a comic book in hand, saw them as, "You two look like you've just seen a ghost."

"Four of 'em," Elliot quipped. "All wearing blue uniforms."

"Huh?" Don responded.

"Are there ghosts here?" Mad asked, fearfully.

"No, honey, no…" Jody went to take her into her arms. "Elliot's just kidding."

Elliot gave Don an *I'll-tell-you-later* look.

And Jody reluctantly supposed she'd better start packing her and Mad's things.

Chapter 18

Don, in his car with Mad, followed Elliot and Jody, in Jody's car. It was a long ride home after a long day. Besides being tired, Don was feeling the turmoil of being both angry and compassionate toward Jody's behavior. Despite it all, he had to laugh again over Elliot's story about the police coming down on him.

On the way out of Duluth he'd picked up a bag of food from McDonald's and munched on it as he drove. Mad, buckled in the passenger seat beside him, was sleeping. He wondered just how much of this crazy event she understood. He supposed Jody's taking her to Duluth had simply meant a fun trip to her. Kids that age probably didn't put too much thought into anything beyond their present moment.

He smiled over at her. What a sweet kid. And what a pity she had the home life she did. How could her mother leave her? And where the heck was her father? And how could her grandmother want to give her away so frivolously? He tried to imagine her as his and Nora's adopted daughter. Yeah, surprisingly he could see it. They could be good for her and her for them. But there was a downside. With Jody feeling the way she did about Mad, he supposed it would seem like they were stealing the child away from her. Funny, how on one side of the picture nobody wanted Mad and on the other side everybody did.

"Oh, Jody…" he spoke his mind aloud. "I sure wish I'd have been there to beat the crap out of Kevin."

"Who's Kevin?" Mad came halfway awake at the sound of Don's voice.

"Nobody. Just some bad guy that should've never been. It's okay. Want a french fry?"

"Sure." Though Mad took one from his bag, she didn't eat it. Before it got to her mouth she was falling back to sleep again.

There was no traffic, making it ultra easy for Don to call Nora on his cell phone. He wanted to let her know that he and Elliot were on their way home with Jody and Mad. He should've phoned her before they left the Skyline, but in the commotion hadn't.

She was relieved to hear from him.

"It'll be late," Don said. "You don't have to wait up for me."

"I want to."

"Okay, I'd like that," he admitted, smiling to himself.

When he hung up from their brief conversation, he looked over at Mad again.

Things are going to get right for you, sweetheart, he assured her in the silence of his mind. *If it can happen for me, it can happen for you.*

* * *

Elliot had insisted on driving Jody's car. He was tired, but she was more tired. To keep his attention sharp he tried keeping a conversation going with her, but it wasn't easy. She seemed talked out and emotionally exhausted. There was just no chit-chat in her. His and Don's showing up as they did had definitely caused her a bad reality crash, and she was suffering with it.

"Y'know," Elliot tried, "sometimes things have to get worse before they get better."

"Am I there yet?" she responded weakly. "At my worst?"

"I don't know. Maybe, yeah. But hey, if you are, then that only means things will get better from here on, right?"

"What makes you think that?"

"Trust me."

"I trusted Kevin. I trusted my stupid fifteen-year old brain. I trusted my dad to be on my side. I don't much trust the word trust."

Elliot poked himself in his chest. "This is me, Elliot. Have I ever let you down? You can trust me, Jody. You know you can."

"I didn't see that when you came barging in on me at the motel."

"No, no…that was *exactly* what you saw in me. I was saving you from yourself. Whether you realize that or not right now, you will in the long run. *Trust me.*"

Jody gave a weary sigh and closed her eyes again.

Elliot gave up on conversation and turned the radio on. Something soft and quiet, so that Jody could rest. She was at an emotional low, but when she felt better she'd see things better.

Slipping frequent glances at her, he kept his thoughts to himself now. Thoughts he'd best keep to himself anyway. Thoughts of how his feelings

The Way Forward

for her had grown into love, or at least something close to it. Her running away like she'd done had scared the wits out of him, causing him to give some serious attention to what she meant to him. He realized he couldn't even imagine his life without her in it anymore. He wanted to be her lifelong protector. He wanted to be her lifelong guy. *Jeez...*he wanted to get up the nerve to tell her these things some day. *Some day.*

When they finally reached Myre, they went first to Don's place where he transferred the still-asleep Mad to Jody's car. He laid her onto the back seat without her even being aware of it. After shutting the door, he paused at Jody's window. She gave him a groggy look and told him thanks. He gave her a thumbs up, turned and walked to his cabin.

"You've got a great brother," Elliot told Jody as he restarted the car.

"I know."

"I mean, especially since you and I got a hold of him and straightened him out last year."

"I know," she said.

From there Elliot drove to Claire's place. He was glad to see a light on. When he lifted Mad out of the back seat, Jody started to get out of the front.

"No," he advised her. "It's best you stay here."

Mad was stirring now and looking through the droopy slits of her eyes, confused at her whereabouts.

"You're home," Elliot told her.

"Where's Jody?"

"In the car."

When they came upon the porch, Elliot set her down on her feet but kept a firm hold of her hand. He knocked on the front door.

When it opened, Claire, in an obvious state of drunkenness, wavered before him. She didn't say anything. It was almost as if she didn't even recognize him. Or Mad.

"Are you okay?" Elliot asked needlessly.

"Wh-what's going on here? Why are you comin' here this time of night?"

"I brought Mad home to you," Elliot said.

Claire tried to focus her gaze on the child. And then it appeared that she was actually trying to focus on the idea of the child even having been gone. She shook her head in confusion. "W-well, I uh...she was in bed last I looked." She reached behind her for her whiskey bottle off an end table.

"*Jeez!*" Elliot said in disgust. "She's been gone for two days, you knew that."

Claire stammered. "W-what day is this?"

"Thursday."

"I don't…I don't understand what she's doing with you. I was just…"

"That's it!" Elliot spun away from Claire. He left the porch with Mad and returned to the car.

Watching him buckle the girl into the back seat, Jody asked in puzzlement what happened.

"We're taking Mad home with us for the night. We'll deal with grandma tomorrow."

When he slipped into the front seat behind the steering wheel, Jody reached over to lay her hand on his arm. It felt to him to be a gesture of trust. Nothing more was said between them. Nothing needed to be.

* * *

As Don and Nora readied for bed in their low-lighted loft room, Don gave her the details of his journey to Duluth and back.

And then she came into his arms, snuggling against him. "I love you. And I love that you care about your sister so much."

"Yeah…like I could wring her neck sometimes."

"An expression of sibling affection if I've ever heard one. You wouldn't feel that way if you didn't truly care about her."

He gave a soft, helpless laugh. "I suppose not."

Next Nora was drawing a kiss out of him. Though he liked it, needed it, and enjoyed it for all its worth, when it ended he immediately returned to the subject of his sister. "I think she feels that she, rather than us, should get Mad."

"Really?"

"I told you about the baby she gave up."

"Yes, and that you think she feels Mad's her replacement."

Don moaned with despair. "Oh…yeah…definitely. She…she's gone off her rocker because of that kid. I mean, running off to Duluth with her like that. Not a smart move. I feel sorry for her, but—"

"But Claire asked *us* to take Mad," Nora reminded him. "I mean, what does Jody really have to offer her? You and I can offer her both parents, a big brother, and a real house soon to come."

"I know that," Don agreed. "But this is something Jody just isn't capable of thinking rationally about."

* * *

The Way Forward

    Jody insisted on putting Mad in her bed instead of on the couch. She helped the girl into her pajamas, that'd been brought in with her bag, kissed her good night, left the room and closed the door.
    When she turned around, with a pillow and blanket in her arms, Elliot was standing there waiting for her.
    "No," he said.
    "No what?" She had no idea what he was referring to.
    "You don't have to sleep on the couch." He took the bedding away from her and tossed it onto the couch in a heap.
    Jody gave him a puzzled look, until he started leading her by the hand toward his room. She stopped and took back her hand. "What's going on?"
    "I know how you're feeling right now," he said. "I know that you're hurting bad. But do you know how I'm feeling? You scared the hell out of me with that running-off-with-Mad stunt. Wondering where your head was. Wondering if you were gone forever. Wondering if you'd get into legal trouble. Wondering if you and Mad were even okay and not in some hospital. Wondering what I'd do if something happened to you. Maybe I just don't want to be alone all night. Maybe you don't either."
    He dipped his head, giving her a persuasive, silent plea.
    Despite the shock of the moment, Jody found herself admitting, "Maybe I don't."
    Elliot took her hand again and continued into his room. "No hanky-pank, I promise. I'd just like us to be close all night for once. Okay?"
    Jody realized that something like this was only bound to happen at some point in their relationship. She just wasn't sure, at this point, if she was ready.
    "Trust me," Elliot added.
    "I do," she said. She motioned behind her to the door. "Can I get my pajamas?"
    "Oh. Yeah. Sure. Go ahead. But…come back."
    She left on a smile and a nod.
    When she returned in her nightclothes, Elliot was already in bed, beneath the covers. Feeling really strange, she crawled into the opposite side.
    After several silent minutes Elliot reached for her and coaxed her over close to him. That was all it took for Jody to break into a hard cry. Tears and sobs came like they'd never quit. With her head nestled against his chest, she could feel his heart beating. His arms held her, like maybe everything could be all right somehow. And she let herself trust in that.
    When her crying finally ceased, Elliot kissed her forehead, said goodnight, and let her go. She slid to her side of the bed, clutching the blankets up tightly.

"It was a stupid thing for me to do, running off with Mad like that," she confessed out of the guilt that had begun where the getaway had failed.

"Very stupid," Elliot agreed, sounding muffled, as if his face was buried in his pillow.

"I'm sorry. Please don't hate me."

"I'll try," he said, jokingly.

"Thank you."

She felt his hand brush against her back, as if it were an accident amidst an innocent movement. Except that he kept it there then, as if wanting continuing proof of their closeness. She wanted it as well.

Chapter 19

The next morning Jody and Elliot left Mad playing in the motel's back yard and Kenny minding the office while they went to talk to Claire. Jody was glad Elliot wanted to go with her and that he did, in fact, agree that the talk was necessary. They'd waited until ten-thirty, allowing Claire some time to deal with the hangover she undoubtedly had.

It'd felt strangely nice to Jody, waking up in Elliot's bed that morning. But also a relief, finding that he'd already risen and was out of there before her. She was glad he'd suggested their sleeping together last night and that sleeping was all he'd intended. Their intimacy had been in holding each other and exchanging some tender and meaningful words. She'd slept like a brick, once her mind had settled down. And upon waking she'd felt blessed with a sense of peacefulness.

When she'd left the bedroom, covering her pajamas with a ratty old robe she found in Elliot's closet, she'd found him in the living room, drinking coffee and watching TV cartoons with Mad. A lovable scene.

When Claire came to the front door, she met Jody and Elliot with a cloud over her head and thunder booming in her voice. "Where's Mad? You've taken her, haven't you! Well, you'd just better—"

"We'd like to come in and talk to you," Jody said.

When she didn't say yes and didn't say no, Jody and Elliot took it upon themselves to open the screen door, walk straight on in past Claire, and seat themselves in the living room.

"Where's my granddaughter?" Claire demanded. "I remembered you took her somewhere. I don't know where. But she ain't back. I checked her room."

"She's at my place," Elliot said. "She's okay."

Claire lowered herself into the armchair across from them. "What do you mean she's okay? Why wouldn't she be? What's been going on here?"

"Maybe if you didn't drink so much," Jody risked saying, "you'd keep better track of her."

Elliot, beside her on the couch, elbowed her from riling Claire any more than she already was if they wanted to try and talk logic with her.

What Jody had really come to say wasn't easy. But it was right. More right than her running off with Mad had been. "What I want to say to you," she began, twisting her hands in her lap, "is that I'd like to adopt Mad."

Claire gave her a long silent look of astonishment before responding. "She's already spoken for. That nice young couple at the bar."

"My brother and his wife."

"Whatever. Yes, I suppose they are."

Trying to keep her cool, Jody continued, "You can give her to me instead."

"No, I'm afraid not," Claire said.

"What difference does it make to you where Mad goes when all that matters to you is to get her off your hands?"

"What matters is you sitting there talking to me like this in my house."

"What matters," Jody exploded, "is that you listen to me!"

Elliot bumped Jody's arm warningly, but she knew there was no other way to talk to this woman except downright bluntly. She did, however, soften her tone. "Look, I've really gotten to know Mad and she's really gotten to know me. I love her. Don and Nora barely know her."

"It's a done deal," Claire stated.

"It doesn't have to be."

"You got no business here, girly, except to return my granddaughter. I'd like you to bring her home. *Now.*"

"Maybe you could just hear Jody out on this," Elliot suggested.

Jody jumped at another chance with Claire. "You know she deserves a better home than this. I would give her one, I promise. That's all you should be concerned with."

Claire glanced around the room, as if she were trying to see it through their eyes.

"It's more about you, Claire, than the house," Elliot clarified to her. "You've got some serious problems of your own, and you know it. And if you aren't willing to take care of yourself you certainly aren't qualified to take care of your granddaughter. I'm vouching that Jody would be perfect for Mad. Use your head, lady. Put your granddaughter into the hands of someone who already knows her, loves her, adores her, and wants her very much."

The Way Forward

"You two…" Claire grumbled, pulling herself up out of her chair, "you just keep at a person no matter what, don't you? You don't listen when you get told something." She walked across the room to fetch her bottle of whiskey off a table.

"Please," Jody begged, blinking her misted eyes.

After taking a drink, Claire gave her a new look. But it wasn't a giving-in sort of look. She'd turned all the harder. "Crying won't work with me."

"She's very emotional," Elliot said of Jody, with obvious emotions of his own crackling in his voice. "And I can assure you she's got a heart bigger than Texas for Mad."

"Texas!" Claire sputtered. "Ain't as big a place as some places I been."

Elliot's mouth tightened, as if he were trying to shut himself up. But it didn't hold and he broke into a shout. "Well, I hope you like *hot* places, lady, because I think that might very well be another place you'll be experiencing some day!"

Now it was Jody who touched his arm in warning as she took over with Claire. "You want to do the right thing, don't you?"

"Don and Nora ain't a mistake. And besides…they're married. You think I want to hand Mad over to a single woman? No. She's had that with her mother and with me. She needs a father in her life now."

Jody felt the painful impact of a whole new strike against her. She stood up from the couch and went over to stand face to face with Claire. "I'm not married, but…but I could be both a father and a mother to her."

Claire shook her head. "I told you no and that's what I mean."

"Please," Jody begged.

Elliot came beside her, grabbing her hand and giving it a yank. "Let's go."

She didn't have the chance to say anything more. Elliot pulled her out of the house, practically on a run, across the porch, down the steps, and out to his car.

"But I wasn't done," Jody wailed resentfully.

"Maybe you weren't, but Claire was. It's no use, Jody. You have to let it go."

She resented his advice. It was so wrong. She couldn't let go. It would be like losing her baby all over again. She wasn't *going* to let go. Not this time.

"Stop the car!" she ordered Elliot on their halfway mark back to the Pinewood.

He gave her a surprised look, caught her level of seriousness, and pulled off the road onto the shoulder.

As soon as the car stopped, Jody was out of it and starting to walk in the direction they'd just come from. Amidst her haste, she called to Elliot, "I need to talk to her some more. Then I'll walk home. You go on. Please. Just go on. Let me do this."

Claire was not happy to see her again. She stood inside the screen door with a *what-now?* look on her face.

Jody was more than anxious to tell her. "If I was married, *then* would you let me…and my husband…adopt Mad?"

Claire gave a crude laugh.

"I mean it," Jody said. "And…and don't think I'd just snatch up a husband out of nowhere. Elliot and I…we've been meaning to get married for some time and we could do it now. We love Mad. We both love Mad. We'd be perfect parents for her. What do you think? Please say yes, Claire. Or at least say you'll give it some thought."

"You are a mighty strange girl, Jody." Claire's laugh actually came softly this time. "And that's a mighty outrageous idea."

"It's not outrageous, it's genuine."

Claire opened the screen door as a gesture for her to come inside. Jody took that as a very good sign. She didn't sit down on this visit. She was too nervous. She stood wringing her hands together, wondering if Claire's going for her whiskey bottle now was another good sign or a bad one. Maybe it was her courage. A woman like Claire needed courage to change her mind about something she'd been so dead set against a few minutes ago.

"So…" Claire began, after a big slug of booze, "you and Elliot are gonna marry, huh?"

"Yes," Jody said with a choke in her voice.

"Why didn't you say so before?"

"I…we…uh…"

"Odd."

"But good, huh? That we'll be married? You said it was the main reason you wanted my brother to take Mad, so she'd have both parents. Now you can consider Elliot and me. *Please* consider Elliot and me."

Claire seemed to be considering. She'd put her bottle down, stood balancing herself against the side of a bookcase, wasn't saying anything, and had a wondrous look on her face.

With her hands behind her back, Jody crossed her fingers in high hope.

Claire took her time. That was good. She should be careful in a decision like this. Jody wanted her to be careful. She wanted Claire to choose *her*.

"Well…" Claire finally broke a long silence, " I guess it'd be okay with me if you and your husband took her, instead of Don and Nora."

"Really?" Jody cried. "You mean it? Oh, Claire, thank you, thank you, thank you. You won't be sorry. And neither will Mad. You'll still be her grandmother. We'll have get-togethers. You'll still be very much part of the picture and—"

"How soon?" Claire interrupted.

The Way Forward

"Excuse me?"

"Are you getting married?" Claire tagged her question.

"Soon, very soon."

"All right then, we'll get to work on adoption arrangements."

Jody cried on her walk to the Pinewood. But it was a happy cry, and a world's difference from a sad cry. She couldn't wait to tell Elliot the news. She…couldn't…wait…to…

Panic was setting in. Her steps became slower and slower until she reached the point of stopping to sit down for a few minutes on a big roadside rock. *Solve one problem, create another,* she made of what she'd done. *Deal with Claire, now with Elliot.* Yet she knew that for as surprised as he was going to be, he'd ultimately be happy that she'd be getting custody of Mad. Happy enough to marry her, she hoped. Her few minutes break stretched to twenty before she felt brave enough to continue her walk.

"Well?" Elliot eagerly met her entrance into the motel office.

"Well what?" she played innocent. "I see Kenny's left, his bike is gone."

"Yes, Kenny's gone. I sent him on an errand. But you're here. And you've just come from another talk with Claire. And you might consider how anxious I am to know how it went."

"It went well," Jody said, heading straight on through to the back room. "She said yes to my getting Mad."

"*What?*" Elliot screeched. He hurried after her and came up beside her where she stood at the door watching Mad in the yard. "The witch said yes? You're kidding! To your getting Mad? Just like that? I don't believe it."

Jody turned toward him, breaking into a laugh over his reaction. And her reaction to his reaction made Elliot pull her into his arms with laughter of his own.

"I don't believe this," he said again, hugging her so tightly that Jody was afraid her deep-down guilt might be squeezed to the surface and openly revealed.

She separated from him just enough to see his face. "There are…"

"What?" he prompted when she paused.

"Conditions," she finished saying.

"Oh, yeah?" Elliot looked curious but unworried. "I suppose there would be some. Of course. I mean, Claire's sure as heck going to make you jump through a few hoops first, right?"

"Something like that."

"Well, let's hear them."

"Later. We'll talk later. I'd like to spend some time with Mad right now."

Jody started out the door to the little girl on the tire swing.

"You're going to tell her already?" Elliot, asked from the doorway.

She spun back to him. "No! And don't you! Not yet!"

"Okay," he said.

Jody continued toward Mad with a smile. Mad unlooped herself from the tire and greeted Jody with a hug.

"I'm really sorry about yesterday," Jody told her for the umpteenth time already that morning. "About the guys coming and spoiling our holiday."

Mad scrinched her face. "I know. That wasn't very nice of them, was it?"

"Absolutely not. But guys…they can act so weird sometimes."

"Yeah." Seemingly undamaged, Mad burst into a giggle.

"I'll make it up to you, honey. I really will."

"That's okay," Mad said with a shrug. "I don't mind coming back. I like it here. I could just be here forever."

Jody's heart was close to bursting. She so wanted to tell Mad that yes, it will be forever. But the time wasn't right yet. There was a lot to straighten out first.

"Why don't you get in the swing," Mad suggested, "and I'll push you."

Jody laughed and did just that. And while in the motion of swooshing back and forth she noticed Elliot standing on the back steps watching. He was one of things that needed straightening. Tonight they would have a talk about getting married.

Chapter 20

Late that afternoon, after Kenny was done for the day and had given Mad a ride home on his bike and Benjamin had arrived for the night shift, Elliot and Jody strolled down the scenic little path to the cottage.

"What's for supper?" Jody asked the master cook.

"Food," came his familiar answer to whenever she asked that question. "But how about we hold off on eating for a while and first pick up our unfinished talk from earlier."

"Sure," Jody agreed easily, then swallowed the lump in her throat.

"Conditions," Elliot reminded her when they were home, sitting together on the couch, shoes off, sipping Cokes, a soft CD playing on the stereo. "You told me there were conditions to your getting Mad…of which you told me we'd talk about later."

She nodded. "I love this CD."

"It now happens to be later," he said.

"It's so romantic."

Elliot gave a little huff. "So you'd rather listen to music than talk?"

"Sorry." She took one more drink of soda then stretched forward to set the can beside his on the coffee table. Then she shifted about, repositioning herself until she was totally sideways, facing Elliot directly, hands fidgeting in her lap.

"Okay, ready?" he asked smartly.

Looking deeply into his eyes, she asked, "Will you marry me?"

Elliot's mouth gapped without words. Not especially the reaction Jody'd hoped for, which made her wish she'd worked up to the proposal more slowly.

When the shock softened he started laughing and it seemed like a yes and she felt better.

Until he crudely uttered, "Where the hell did *that* come from?"

She'd surely hoped the romantic song on the stereo would offer enough ambiance to help her through this. But for the way it was going, it seemed not. She cozied against him and put her arms around his neck.

"Jody..." he began cautiously, "what's going on here?"

"I just proposed to you."

"Well, yeah...I know...but..."

She put her lips to his. A kiss was something he could better understand, and he instantly got into it without needing any explanation. He took it so well that he was reluctant to let it end when Jody started drawing back.

Wow. As they sat staring at one another, Jody had to tell herself it'd only been a kiss. But she couldn't tell herself why she'd felt such a strong sexual arousal amidst it, or why she'd seen fireworks behind her closed eyes.

Elliot, sitting there in his own state of amazement, said out loud the same word that was in her mind. "*Wow.*"

"I know..." she agreed.

"Did you feel that?" he eagerly asked her.

"Yes."

When Elliot started closing in for a replay, Jody stopped him.

Grasping his head between his hands, he shot up from the couch bellowing, "What are you trying to do to me here, Jody?"

She offered only a meek smile.

He stressed his frustration, "Out of the blue you ask me to marry you, then you kiss me like there's no tomorrow, then when I get excited you give me the cold shoulder."

"I'm sorry," she said.

"You're *sorry?*" His eyes narrowed at her. "About...the proposal, the kiss, your sudden rejection, or your driving me crazy?"

"It's the condition," she said.

He shrugged, giving her a duh look.

"The proposal, it's the condition."

He remained stupefied.

Jody stood up before him, placing her hands tenderly against his chest and looking him straight in the eye, intent on getting through to him.

He backed away from her. "Hey...no...if you're gonna try seducing me again, you'd better do it like you mean it."

She sank back down onto the couch. He was right. He deserved a straighter explanation, minus any sexual distractions. "I went back to talk to Claire again."

"Right. I know that much." Elliot sat down beside her.

The Way Forward

"Her main reason for giving Mad to Don and Nora instead of me was that they were a married couple and Mad would have both parents. So…"

"*Jeez!*" He slapped himself in the forehead. "Okay, I'm getting it. In order for you to get Mad you have to marry me?"

"Yes."

"Last night…after everything…I really thought you'd come to your senses. Now I'm thinking that may be an impossibility."

"I…I thought you'd like the idea of marrying me."

"Do I seem like a marrying sort of guy to you, Jody? I mean, jeez I tried it once and it didn't work. If I'd have ever considered it again, with you, I'd have asked you long before this."

"So you're turning me down," she concluded, feeling panicked and hurt. And then she honestly had to wonder which hurt the most…his rejection to marriage or her losing the chance to adopt Mad.

"I'm…not…turning you down," he denied nervously. "I'm just trying to feel my way through the shock of it."

"Then you'll marry me?"

"I didn't say that."

"Fine," she snapped, losing what was left of her hope and her nerve

"Where you going?" he said to her back as she left the cottage.

She didn't answer. She didn't know.

It was dark out when Jody stopped driving around aimlessly and found herself parking before Don's cabin. She hadn't intended to go there but somehow, to her own amazement, she'd ended up there. She wasn't sure she wanted to face her brother, but the lights glowing in the cabin windows were inviting.

* * *

Aware of a car pulling into his driveway, Don opened the cabin door to have a look. He was both surprised and troubled, seeing that it was Jody.

"Can I come in?" she asked, stepping up to the door.

"Sure." He opened the way for her, immediately detecting her low spirit.

"Hi, Jody," Nora greeted her entrance to the kitchen area.

"Hey, Jody," Kenny called to her from the living room area.

Unresponsive to both of them, Jody sat down at the table. Don and Nora exchanged looks, waiting for her to explain her unexpected visit.

"We had a fight," she finally disclosed.

"You and Elliot?" Don verified.

She nodded.

Don took the chair across from her, grinning with disbelief. "Come on, you two? No way. What about?"

Nora, standing beside him, poked him as in letting him know he shouldn't have asked.

"I don't want to talk about it," Jody let him know as well.

"Then why'd you come here?" Don boldly put it to her.

Nora poked him harder this time, then pleasantly offered Jody, "Would you like some coffee or tea?"

"No thanks," Jody said, looking as though she appreciated another woman's perception. "I'm all right, really. I…I just needed to get out a little…and…"

"You guys seemed good together when I left the motel this afternoon," Kenny remarked, coming into the kitchen area.

"Please," Nora told him, flicking her hand at him, "go back to what you were doing. You're not part of this conversation."

"Sorry," he said, leaving. Then probably realizing he would still be within earshot, he returned. "Why don't I just take the dog for a walk," he suggested, *like they really had one.*

"Good idea," Don responded to the boy's witticism.

Kenny left the cabin on a good-natured laugh.

"So…" Don turned his focus back on Jody, "what can we do for you?"

The phone rang and he moaned at the interruption but got up to answer it. It was Elliot.

"I'm kinda beside myself here. Jody's taken off again. She's been gone for hours and I—"

"She's here," Don told him before he went any further.

"She is?" Elliot gasped with relief.

"She's sitting at our kitchen table, crying."

"Oh," Elliot's voice dropped.

"She says you guys had a fight."

"Ah, well…yeah, sort of."

"A *fight*, Elliot. She's shook up and crying."

"Tell her I'm sorry."

"Why don't you just get your butt over here and tell her yourself."

"I…I could do that. Keep her there. Don't let her go, okay?"

"She'll be here."

"Meanwhile…" Elliot added hastily, "give her a message from me."

"Stupid, if you're coming here anyway. But okay."

"Tell her I said yes. That I accept."

"You accept," Don verified, frowning at having no idea to what it referred to.

The Way Forward

Elliot laughed. "Yeah, when the shock wore off I came around to feeling okay about our having to get married. See you in a few. Bye."

Don hung up the phone and turned around with a whole new look at his baby sister.

"I don't want to see him!" she said.

Don felt sorry for Jody and madder than hell at Elliot. And no, he wasn't going to relay Elliot's message to her. And no, he certainly wasn't going to let him in when he got there. The two of them having had a little fight had now become something way more. Elliot's getting Jody pregnant was going to cost him a punch in the nose, to say the least.

Chapter 21

When Elliot pulled into Don's driveway, he felt nicely welcomed by Don's running out to greet him. Until Don got nearer.

"You sonofabitch!" Don shouted.

Elliot got out of his car and held up his hands defensively. "What? What's this about? Back off, okay?"

Don unclenched his fists and leaned against the car. "You *know* what it's about."

"Like I'd be asking?" Elliot differed.

"It's about your taking advantage of my sister, that's what it's about!"

Elliot shook his head in puzzlement. "Jody? What do mean?"

Kenny, with obvious concern, came strolling back to the cabin amidst the guys' argument, asking, "What's going on?"

"That's what I'd like to know," Elliot said.

"Do you mind, Kenny?" Don shot him down at his presence. "You're not part of this conversation."

"Sure. I'll just get lost again. See ya." He took off out of the yard and down the road.

Another puzzlement Elliot didn't get. "Come on, Don. Why are you pissed at me? I think I've got a right to know."

"If you need it spelled out, it's about Jody's being pregnant."

"*What?*" Elliot shrieked.

Don stepped away from the car. "Don't play dumb with me. It's not cute."

Elliot held up his hands again. "I'm dumb, I swear to you, I'm dumb. I didn't know anything about this. Really. *Jeez*. I don't belive it! I had no idea that—"

Don started to make a lunge for him, then stopped with reconsideration. "Truth?"

The Way Forward

Elliot now held up just one hand…his *honest-to-God* hand. "I swear. *Jeez.* Yes. I didn't know anything about this. And if there *is* a this, I'm not a part of it."

Finally paying better attention to him, Don said, "Well, I guess I'm sorry then. But I'm also damned confused."

"Me too. Pregnant? No, I don't think so. If Jody's in a delicate condition, I think it strictly pertains to Mad."

"Mad? What about her? What's she got to do with this?"

Elliot took hold of Don's arm, very gently so's to not set him off, and led him over to the cabin steps. "We need to talk."

The guys sat in the dark, peacefully now and with softer voices. Elliot told Don about Jody's desperation to adopt Mad and the deal she made with Claire in order to win that privilege."

At first Don was ultra serious, but eventually he wound up laughing. "Man, what cereal box did my sister get her brain out of? First she kidnaps Mad. Then she tries to step ahead of Nora and me for adoption rights. Then she promises Claire she'll marry you as part of the deal. Then topping it all off, it sounds like you turned down her proposal."

Elliot laughed as well. "Yeah, it is all kind of funny, isn't it…in a horrendous sort of way."

"And then you changed your mind about marrying her? Like now you want to?"

"Yeah. I guess it's about time anyway. I've felt the transition happening for some time now, our relationship growing from casual to serious."

Don nodded. "Sexual."

"Not quite. A couple kisses. That's it. Honest."

"But my kid sister…she turns you on?"

"Yeah," Elliot admitted, man-to-man. "And you don't know how difficult it's been sometimes for me to resist the temptation."

"But you're a gentleman," Don said assuredly.

"More like an idiot. Anyway, after the shock of Jody's proposal wore off, I knew I'd give her a yes when she got back. But when she didn't come back I got worried and that's when I called you."

"Man, oh, man…" Don made of the event.

"I know," Elliot sighed.

* * *

Aware of Don and Elliot being outside on the steps, Jody and Nora patiently waited for them to come inside. But when the time began to run long, Jody decided, "I'm going out there."

Nora told her, "You don't have to. If you want Elliot to leave, Don and I will make him do so."

"Thanks, but maybe it should be me who tells him to leave."

The guys looked behind them when the cabin door opened. Elliot jumped to his feet, giving Jody a smile she didn't want.

"I don't know why you bothered coming over here," she scowled at him, "but you shouldn't have. And you can leave again right now."

Elliot was surprised. "Don didn't give you my message?"

"No, I never did," Don confessed.

Jody gave her brother an adamant look. "What message?" Then she shot the same look at Elliot. "What message?"

Don got to his feet, tossing his hands. "*You* guys duke it out. Come on, Nora, lets go inside."

They went into the cabin, closing the door behind them.

"Oh, Jody..." Elliot said apologetically, "c'mere." He motioned for her to sit down with him on the step. "Everything's gone so crazy."

"Especially you," she quipped.

"Yeah, at first," he agreed. "Until I changed my mind. That message you didn't get was my *yes*."

Jody squinted at him, doubtful of her hearing.

But he verified it with a nod. "I want to marry you. Yes! But *jeez, girl...* you kind of took me by surprise, y'know? And then you barely gave me a chance to react rationally before you blew out of there. It's not every day a guy gets proposed to. After you left, it didn't take me long to think *yeah, okay, what the hell*."

Jody sat there gathering in his side of the story while feeling ashamed of hers. "I was wrong, using you behind your back to make a deal with Claire."

"Yeah," he agreed.

"And I was even more wrong to...to just assume that you'd *want* to marry me."

"No, no...you're wrong about feeling wrong there. Like where else are we supposed to go with our long-standing relationship if not to get married? Your springing this on me was the wake-up call I needed. I want to marry you, Jody. I think I've wanted to for a long time but have been too afraid to admit it."

She smiled at him. "Are you still afraid?"

"Scared as hell. But it's a happy sort of scared. Know what I mean?"

She smiled again. "Yes."

"There's been some reluctance on your part, too, toward our getting serious, right?"

"Yes."

"Until now. Until Claire actually said she'd make arrangements for you to adopt Mad if you were married to me."

"Yes. Simple as that."

"*Simple*," he teasingly overstated the term. "Yeah…okay…maybe. But y'know, for as serious as this has supposedly come, you and I, we've still never exchanged the "L" word."

"Have you *felt* the "L" word?" she asked with a grin.

"I have. Have you?"

"Yes."

"Let's make it official."

"Okay."

"At the same time, on the count of three."

"Okay."

Elliot gave the count, and on three they both said at the same time to each other, "I love you."

"There…" he said, "now we have a real basis for marriage."

"I mean it, you know…about loving you."

"I know. And I mean it too, Jody, from the bottom of my heart. But before we get married I have a condition for *you* to meet."

She was afraid to ask, but before she could he told her. "We have to exchange another kiss just as good as the one we had earlier at the cottage."

She relaxed, finding the condition reasonable. "I think I can meet that. I think we might even be able to beat it."

"Start beating," he said, pulling her into his arms.

One kiss turned into another and another and another. Until something interrupted them.

A voice called from somewhere in the outer darkness. It was Kenny, asking, "Okay if I come home now?"

* * *

"Are you disappointed?" Nora asked Don over breakfast the next morning.

Deep in his own thoughts at the moment, he wasn't sure what she was referring to.

"About Mad," she clarified. "About Jody getting her and not us?"

"Oh, uh, no…well, maybe a little. You?"

"I'm disappointed, but more importantly I'm happy for Jody."

Don nodded. "I know what Mad means to her. Anyway," he said, munching a spoonful of cereal, "we've got Kenny."

Nora left her chair, came around to his side of the table, wrapped her arms around his neck, and kissed the top of his head. "You're a good brother. And husband. And stepfather."

"I agree to all of the above," Kenny said, joining them. He'd had his cereal in the living room area and came now to put his empty bowl in the sink.

"We've gotta get a bigger house," Don stated teasingly. "Man, this kid has big ears."

"Yeah, yeah..." Kenny drawled. "Only because of the subject matter going on around here. Anyway, thanks for filling me in on everything last night after Jody and Elliot left. I'm disappointed, too, about not getting Mad for my little sister. But maybe down the line you guys will make that happen for me in a more natural sort of way."

Nora snapped him with a dishtowel.

"Well, if you do..." he called from his return to the living room, "I think I'd really rather have a brother."

Don gave Nora a seductive look. "We'll see what we can do, right?"

"When we get a bigger house," she said.

"And a more private bedroom," Don added.

Chapter 22

One week after Jody's proposal, Mr. and Mrs. Treggor, wearing matching wedding bands and dress-up clothes, sat having a lunch in a nice restaurant in downtown Duluth. They'd been married by a justice of the peace two hours ago, and this was the beginning of their honeymoon.

"We did it!" Elliot said, bursting with amazement. "We really did it!"

Jody grinned at him. "Scared?"

"Yes."

"Me too," she admitted. "Happy?"

"Yes, yes, yes! And I guess I have Mad to thank for this."

"Let's not blame all of this on her," Jody laughed. "I'd like to take some credit."

Tilting his head to one side, his eyes twinkled at her. "Then I guess I have *you* to thank. And I will, believe me, tonight."

Jody twisted her wedding ring around on her finger. Despite her happiness, she had to wonder, "This isn't wrong, is it, our getting married this way? I mean...aren't we being as hasty as Don was?"

Elliot considered it a weak comparison. "Don knew Nora two weeks. You and I have known each other three years."

"I mean, we've never talked about getting married until recently."

Elliot covered her ring hand with his ring hand. "That doesn't mean we haven't thought about it in our own ways, right?"

Jody smiled at the truth of it.

He squeezed her hand. "You'd be surprised at some of the thoughts I've had about you...*us*...over the years."

"Really?"

"Come on...you've had them, too, I know you have."

"Thoughts?" she questioned playfully.

"Like the ones you're getting right now," he said, reading her closely and correctly.

"Dessert?" the waiter was suddenly beside them offering.

"Uh…no thanks," Elliot said. "We're leaving now. We're in kind of a hurry, so if we could just get the check, please."

The waiter nodded and left, and Jody giggled at Elliot's urgency.

Elliot shook his finger at her while making a dramatic proclamation. "This isn't funny, my dear. I may sound confident about our wedding night, but the fact is I'm *scared to death*."

"Oooh…" she cooed, "don't be. I'll be right there with you."

"That's what I'm scared of."

Jody reached across the table and slugged him.

"See why?" he squawked.

The waiter returned with the check. "Is everything all right here?"

"Yes," Elliot exclaimed proudly, "very all right!"

From the restaurant they went to the Skyline Motel, which they now labeled as their regular place. Elliot had phoned ahead to book a room.

The desk clerk recognized them the moment they entered the office and held up a warning hand. "We don't want any trouble here, please."

"Just our room," Elliot said, stepping up to the counter.

The clerk was still looking back and forth between them skeptically when Jody held out her hand to show him her wedding band. "It's okay. We're married."

"But…but isn't he the one who…well, didn't he…?

"The cops cleared me that night, remember?" Elliot said. "*Jeez*."

Despite his hesitance, the clerk nevertheless checked them in. But as Elliot and Jody started up the stairway, each carrying a bag, he called to them, "I don't want any trouble."

"Neither do I," Elliot responded. Then grinning at Jody, he asked her, "You're not going to give me any trouble, are you?"

She giggled. "I don't think I can promise that."

"That's my Jody," he said.

When they got to their assigned room on the second floor, Elliot unlocked the door, opened it, set the luggage inside, then turned back for his bride. He swooped Jody up into his arms, carried her over the threshold, then bumped the door shut with his foot.

He kissed her once while she was in his arms, then again after putting her down.

The Way Forward

When Jody had a chance to look about, she realized, "It's the same room. It's the one we shared last year when we were on our way to find Don. Elliot…you asked specifically for it, didn't you?"

"Specifically. Except we won't be needing both beds this time." He took her back into his arms. "I love you, Jody. I think I've always loved you, even before I knew you."

"That's nice. Silly, but nice."

"Just like you," he said. Then he caught her up-raised hand just before it struck him. "Can't you think of anything better to do to your husband other than hitting him?"

"I've got a few ideas, yes."

"Good."

They headed toward one of the beds together.

Three days later Elliot carried Jody over another threshold, the one to the cottage. The reality of their being husband and wife was becoming more believable day by day, and Jody was loving the transition more than she would've ever imagined.

Being married certainly hadn't hampered Elliot's humor. At this especially endearing moment, he quipped, "You're sure Claire promised you custody of Mad if I married you and that this isn't just a trick?"

"Too late to wonder now," she giggled, as he put her down.

"Hey, you know what?" he settled on. "I'm lovin' it for *whatever* reason!"

"And you know I love this little place," she said, looking around the house with the newness of having been away from it for more like a year rather than a few days. "I suppose it will be a bit small, with Mad here, too. But I'd sure hate to think of moving."

"We won't have to move," he said. "I like this place, too. And it's pretty darn handy to the motel. There's plenty of room out back, and we can easily build on if we want."

"Really?" she squealed with delight.

"No, I'm lying."

She laughed and punched his arm.

"Hey…" he moaned, "don't little girls stop doing that once they get married?"

"I'm not a little girl."

"Sorry. No. I absolutely know that you're not a little girl. Mrs. Treggor, you are one beautiful, sexy lady."

"Tell me…" she said, cozying up to him, "do beautiful, sexy ladies still have to do cleaning and laundry and grocery shopping and—"

"Yes."

"Oh," she sighed, pretending to be disappointed. Only to hopefully add, "But you'll still do the cooking, right?"

"Right."

"I'm hungry."

"Me too."

"So what are you making?"

He slowly and seductively urged her toward the bedroom. "How about love? I'm hungry for making love right now. Wanna join me?"

She smiled a yes at him, then said, "How come it took so long for us to realize we were in love?"

"I don't know," he said, "but it's sure fun making up for lost time."

*   *   *

The steady morning mist turned into a hard downpour by mid day and brought a hault to Don's outside work. He stopped in at Maxy's, surprising Nora and sitting down at the bar to order a Coke.

"What are you doing here?" she badgered him playfully.

"Raining out. Can't work in the rain."

"So…does this mean you're going to just sit here and bug me the rest of the day?"

"You bet. Can't think of a more fun way to spend a rainy afternoon."

They kissed across the counter. Then Don told her, "I heard from Jody. She called my cell phone earlier. She and Elliot are back from their honeymoon. It still doesn't compute with me that my little sister's married." He laughed ahead of adding, "I still can't believe that *I'm* married."

"Things are changing pretty fast around here, aren't they," Nora concluded. "Even the fact that Kenny's off somewhere with this new girlfriend he's already acquired. They went to Duluth for the day with her mother. "

"Some date," Don sneered.

"A *safe* one, wouldn't you say?"

"Some date," Don belittled it again.

A scruffy looking guy wandered into Maxy's and over to the bar. He ordered a whiskey straight up. Then he stood drinking it while studying Don.

"Do we know each other?" Don finally asked him.

"I know who you are," the guy said, "but I don't guess we really know each other. Not like your wife and I know each other."

"Huh?" Don asked, though wasn't sure he wanted a repeat of what he thought he'd heard.

"Just saying that I don't know you like I know your wife."

The Way Forward

Don turned his head to Nora. She looked a little nervous, but didn't say anything one way or the other.

The guy told Don, "You ain't the first one around here who's gotten to know Missy Nora."

"What's that mean?" Don asked.

"It means just what it means. Nora and me, we was seeing each other for a while before you started coming here. Weren't we, Nora?"

Don looked at her again. The look on her face seemed to indicate some guilt, and he was starting to feel sick.

"We was real close, too," the scruffy one stated. "*Real* close, weren't we Nory?"

"That's enough, Wally," she warned him.

"No, it's okay, I'd like to hear more," Don said in anquish.

"No, you wouldn't," Nora assured him. "Because it was nothing, believe me."

Wally took a stool. "Guess we're embarrassing her, huh?" he said in a buddy-buddy manner to Don. "Despite that, yeah I'd be glad to tell you more about this. Another whiskey, Nora," he interrupted himself. Then back to Don, he continued, "Her car wouldn't start one night after closing. I happened to still be here and on the way out myself. I offered to give her a ride home and she accepted."

Don was eyeing Nora while listening to Wally.

"Then, guess what?" Wally continued joyously. "When I was going to leave her place, *my* car wouldn't start. Must'a been a car virus going around that night. Anyway, I'd had a lot to drink, and all in all Nora was kind enough to let me come in and sleep it off on her couch. Nice girl, this Nory. *Very* nice. And she was mighty grateful to me for getting her home that night. Mighty grateful, if you know what I mean."

Don didn't like the wink Wally tacked onto his story. Nor did he like the story. Nor did he like that it was raining outside, which put him out of work, which influenced him to stop in at Maxy's and surprise his wife. Nor did he like that he was the one who got the biggest surprise out if it. He swiveled from side to side on his stool, feeling sorry for himself, resentful of Nora, and pure hatred for this Wally jerk.

As Wally continued on and on about Nora's amazing gratefulness toward him, Don finally interrupted with a dreaded thought, "Are you roundaboutly trying to tell me that you and she had sex together that night?"

Wally raised his bushy eyebrows. "What do you think? Huh? Just what do you think?"

"I think no."

Wally laughed. "Well then you're just about the stupidest guy I've ever known. Any woman who tends bar and deals with guys like me is one easy—"

Don rose from his stool and in one continuous motion plunged into Wally. He knocked him clean off his stool and sent him stumbling to the floor. Don dropped down onto him and started hitting.

"Stop it!" Nora shouted, coming out from behind the bar.

Max from the back room also came running to the sound of the ruckus. He grabbed Don and pulled him off Wally. "Stop it! What the hell's going on here?"

Wally got to his feet, happy to explain. "The guy asked to hear a story and when I started telling it he got violent."

"What's the matter with you, Don? You had too much to drink or—"

"He doesn't drink," Nora told her boss.

"Well, stop acting like you do," Max ordered him. "Behave yourself or I'll have to make you leave."

Immediately after Max had gone back to his office, Wally turned obnoxious again. "Come to think of it…" he added to Don, ignoring the fact that they'd just tangled, "the timing of that night I'm referring to…it actually sort of happened *after* you and Nora had started dating."

Don flared up again, on the verge of another fight.

"Sorry," Wally apologized, short of sincerity. "But I guess we all know that those things just sort of happen…I mean, with women who tend bar."

"Leave!" Nora told him. "You have no business talking like this, leading Don to believe that you and I—"

"You're just regretting not having told him about this before I did, right, honey? And you guys call yourself married, with secrets like this between you? Shame on you."

He staggered out of the bar, laughing to himself all the way.

"I'll have a vodka straight up," Don told Nora, slapping his hand onto the counter.

"No you won't, " she said.

"Vodka straight up," he said again, louder.

"You don't drink, remember? And you're not going to start now over something stupid like this."

"Something stupid like this is *exactly* why I'm going to start. Now if you won't serve me here, I'll drive the ten miles to Dale's liquor store and get my own. A whole damn fifth of vodka."

"Don, please." She leaned across the countertop to him. "You've told me about your past drinking problem. And you told me how proud you were of giving it up. Don't spoil that. Wally's a drunk who runs off at the mouth like a drunk. Don't let him upset you."

"Maybe it's not him who's upsetting me. Maybe it's you."

"There was nothing to it, that night. "

The Way Forward

"Then how come you never told me about it?"

"Because *there was nothing to it.* Now knock it off. You're scaring me."

"And you're scaring me."

"Listen…he drove me home and yes, his car broke down. It's an old rattletrap. And yes, he was drunk and I suggested he sleep it off on my couch. But no, we didn't have sex. He kissed me, but—"

"Kissed you?" Don felt a weird sort of satisfaction in catching her.

"That's probably what he was referring to when he inferred something happened. A kiss. A meaningless kiss. And the only reason there was one was because he caught me off guard, grabbed me and kissed me before I knew what was happening. His idea. Bad idea. For which I slapped him hard across the face, threw him a blanket, went to my room, slammed the door and locked it. When I got up the next morning, he was gone. Somehow his clunker started and he left."

"I'll have my vodka now, please," Don insisted.

"In his warped mind," Nora said, "I guess he liked pretending we'd been close that night. But I think you know me better than that."

Don stood up. "Well, I can see that I'm not going to get served here." He started for the door.

"Don, stop it!" Nora shouted after him. "Don't be crazy! You've got no reason to—"

He was outside, in the rain, going for his car, feeling that he deserved to be crazy if he wanted to be. He had all the reason in the world to seek an escape. Krista had hurt him bad years ago. Maybe, he was thinking now, that it was just something that all women did to you. Maybe trying to be a nice guy didn't mean anything to them. Maybe it even made it easier for them to abuse him. Well, *shit!*

It was as dark inside the cabin, where Don sat later, as it was outside. He sat at the table, listening to the incessant rain beyond the screen door. It was the only sound he heard. He liked it that way. Just him and the dark and the rain. It was soothing. Just him and the dark and the rain and his bottle of vodka before him.

Nora surprisingly came home earlier than the end of her shift, hurrying inside as if she were approaching an emergency. Maybe this was one, Don thought, though he wondered *was it hers or his?*

"Don!" she said at the relief of finding him, although she must have seen his car outside.

"Yeah," he answered, "it's me."

"I've been so worried about you. Max finally let me off early. Don…" She saw the bottle of booze before him.

He let her worry a minute longer. Then he told her, "I didn't open it. I went all the way to Dale's to get it and bring it home, but I didn't open it."

Good," she sighed, further relieved.

"I've just been sitting here looking at it."

"It's your demon, that bottle."

"I know."

"And Wally was another demon, which you didn't manage to handle as well."

Don gave her a sullen look.

"What was I supposed to have done?" Nora asked. "Wally almost went off the road driving me home that night. Should I have just sent him on his way to his own place after dropping me off? Probably. I don't know. But I didn't. Excuse me, but I was worried about him."

"You're a kind person," Don gave her.

"Yes, kind, but not easy."

Don gave her a smile. "Except with me."

"Except with you," she admitted.

Don turned sideways on the chair and pulled her onto his lap. "I'm sorry for loosing it like that earlier, Nora. I'm sorry for believing him over you. I'm sorry I scared you."

"And I'm sorry I never mentioned that stupid incident to you before. It just wasn't—"

"It's okay," he said. "Really, I'm okay about it now. And I don't need a drink of vodka, Nora, I just need you."

She got up, grabbed the bottle of vodka off the table, marched it over to the sink, broke the seal, unscrewed the top, and dumped the contents down the drain. Then she came back to Don's lap, assuring him, "You've *got* me."

Chapter 23

Jody stood a long time at the back screen door of the motel break room, quietly day dreaming and watching Mad on the tire swing. Elliot was at the cottage, repairing the leaky kitchen faucet. It'd been two weeks since their wedding, and Jody was liking her new world more and more each day. Though Elliot was still Elliot, he seemed sweeter and somehow more genuine than she'd ever known him to be. So many dreams were coming true, and so many more were in production.

When she heard the front office door open, it indicated the end of her break and she went to tend business.

The customer was a young woman, alone and without a suitcase or a purse. She wore a denim skirt and a white blouse and appeared to be rather nervous.

Despite a sinking feeling coming to Jody about this woman, she greeted her pleasantly. "Good-morning. You'd like a room?"

"No room," she said, giving both the office and Jody a once-over. "Are you Jody Mitchell?"

"Treggor," Jody said. "It's Jody Treggor now. Excuse me, but should I know you?"

"Our phone conversation…yes."

Jody's intuition had been correct. "Susan," she spoke the woman's name outwardly, despite hating the sound of it, and who it represented, and the fact that she was standing right here in the Pinewood office.

The visitor nodded, needlessly verifying, "Madison's mother."

Jody's world crashed. She stuck her hands on her hips. "Well, this is one heck of a big shock, you're showing up like this!"

The Susan woman was surprised at Jody's outburst. "We talked on the phone and—"

"And you didn't seem that interested in your daughter's welfare at that time."

"And I must say that you seemed a little *overly* interested in it," Susan threw back at her. "Which I still don't get. But you're wrong about me. Of course I was interested hearing about Maddy. Maybe just not from a stranger. And what you didn't know was that actually I was planning on making this trip soon anyway."

Jody swallowed the lump in her throat. "*Were* you?"

"Look," Susan said firmly, "I'm not sure what your part is in this, other than being a neighbor, but—"

"It's pretty strong," Jody assured her.

"When you called, I admit I might've seemed a little resentful, but—"

"Right," Jody snapped. "Like why would you want to hear anything about your daughter?"

"But after the initial shock of your call settled, it didn't take me long to feel appreciative. Your call…it inspired me to move up the time of my trip."

"This trip, so what does it mean?" Jody asked, in spite of knowing.

"I've come for Maddy."

Jody shook her head. "No."

"No?" Susan questioned.

"You've lost your right to her."

"She's my daughter."

"You're too late."

"What do you mean I'm—"

Elliot burst through the front door, sputtering, "Can't fix the damn thing without a certain part I need. I'm going to have to— *Ooops.*" He stopped upon realizing he'd interrupted something.

Jody made forced introductions. "This is Elliot, my husband. Elliot, this is Susan, Mad's mother."

Elliot's mouth dropped in awe. He gave the woman a stiff nod, and then his gaze flicked back to Jody in disbelief.

Jody met his reaction with, "Yeah! Can you imagine that?"

"Y-Yes and no," he said awkwardly.

"She thinks she can just waltz in here like nothing's happened!" Jody scowled.

"Okay, okay…" Elliot tried to calm her.

"But a *lot* has happened."

"Okay, okay…" Elliot said again. "I agree, but just settle down and maybe we can talk about this."

"I don't see that there's anything to talk about," Jody stated bitterly.

"You thought so when you phoned me," Susan reminded her.

The Way Forward

"That was then, this is now. So maybe you'd just better turn around and—"

"I understand she hangs out here all the time," Susan said. "So is she here now?"

Jody had the urge to run out back, grab Mad's hand, take off with her and never look back. Instead she found herself asking Susan a stupid, emotionally loaded question. "Why?"

"I'm her mother, that's why," the woman responded, as if it were the obvious answer to a riddle.

"I thought you were out of the picture," Elliot boldly put it to her.

Susan looked at him as if he, too, spoke in riddles. "Is a mother *ever* out of the picture?"

Jody felt hit by the truth of it being *no. Once a mother, always a mother.* Except she didn't want it to apply to Susan. Maybe at first, with the phone call, but not now. Not today. "It's just so strange," she said, feeling her spirit spiraling down, "your showing up at this particular time."

Since Susan didn't get the significance of her timing, Elliot asked her, "Claire didn't tell you about the adoption plans?"

From Susan's bewildered look, it seemed not. But she had her own plan. "I'm here to get my daughter back. I think I've got some pretty good grounds that'll work toward that. One being, I'm engaged to my psychologist."

Jody saw Elliot slip a quick grin. Though the psychologist association did seem rather comical first off, she took it to more seriously mean that Susan's impending marriage to him would definitely and conveniently award her some real points toward getting Mad back. It certainly wouldn't hurt any that she'd be marrying a certified psychologist, not to mention, to begin with, that she was the child's biological mother. Jody was feeling whipped in a battle beyond her control.

"Do you have kids?" Susan asked her.

Jody drew a deep breath and let it out on, "Elliot and I...we just got married."

"Congratulations."

Jody said nothing. Saying thank you to this woman for anything at all at this moment was beyond her means.

"Susan," Elliot began, making like some high-class lawyer, "are you aware of how much your mother drinks? If you are, you could be charged for leaving your daughter in her care. And if you weren't aware of it, that could only be another irresponsible oversight of yours."

Susan answered morosely, "Funny...that despite my own alcohol addiction and how it messed up my life and lost me my daughter, yeah, of course I knew my mother drank. But I didn't know how much until now.

Or maybe, back then, I didn't *want* to know because she was the only one, the only relative available to take Madison. I didn't want Maddy to go to a stranger. As my brain slowly dried out in rehab, I came to realize that Mom probably wasn't much better at taking care of her than I'd been. I'm well now and Mom's not, which is definitely another of my grounds toward *getting Maddy back*."

"So your drinking…" Elliot said, "that's what got you sent up."

"I wasn't in *prison*," Susan responded sharply. "I was in rehab for my disease. And…" she added, "for…for some behavioral problems I'd assumed along with it. Oh, I never hurt Madison. Not physically. But I…I'm sure she was scared a lot of the time. I went away. And paid for my mistakes. And got myself well. And now I'm trying to live down my stupidity, and I just want to make up for it the best I can."

Jody and Elliot exchanged sickly looks. Of the two of them, Jody was sure she was the sickest. Possibly dying. She needed to sit down. She went to the bench by the front window. Susan came to sit beside her. *Damn*…she didn't want to be this close to the woman. She didn't even want to acknowledge that this woman existed. *Go away. Please go away. I'm sorry I called you. It's too late for you to get Mad back. You can't have her back. God, this hurts.*

While Jody was on the verge of tears, her closer look at the woman beside her found that Susan was already shedding some. What did Susan have to cry about? Hadn't her heart been too cold for too long to behave like this now? More yet, hadn't she just spoken confidently about getting Mad back?

Jody watched the mother of Mad dab her eyes with a Kleenex. The tears were wet enough to be real. They even drew Jody's sympathy away from herself and toward Susan.

Susan sweetly apologized. "I'm sorry for falling apart like this, but you wouldn't believe what I've gone through to even get this far."

Jody felt touched. She didn't *want* to feel touched. Not for Mad's mother. Not since for some time *she'd* come to feel like Mad's mother. At least by way of the unavoidable comparison she couldn't help making between Mad and the daughter she herself had lost and would give anything in the world to be reunited with. It hurt. And it was ironic that in addition to her own hurt she was sitting here helplessly understanding Susan's hurt. But then, how could she humanly not?

When Jody put her hand on Susan's arm and patted it, Susan gave her a warm thank-you smile. Jody realized that there was no way she could hate this woman for what she'd done and was now doing. She was a mother, yearning for her child, and there was no stronger need than that in the whole world.

When Jody looked across the room at Elliot, he frowned, shrugged and shook his head dumbfoundedly. She didn't blame him, as she herself barely

The Way Forward

grasped her own turnabout. A moment ago she'd been close to throwing this woman out on her ear, and now she was sitting here relenting to her.

"I'm sorry," Susan said again, her voice steadier now. "You're being very considerate to me, despite what you must think of me."

"You're Mad's mother," Jody simplified the judgement.

"It's such a long story," Susan agonized.

"Especially to a seven-year old," Elliot scoffed.

Jody popped up from the bench, giving him a sharp look that said, *shut up*. Then she looked back at Susan, which felt almost as if she were looking in the mirror for all they had in common. Feeling newly protective of this woman, she offered to her, "Things happen. Sometimes bad things to good people. We all have our stories. It doesn't mean wrongdoings can't be mended."

Susan shifted her position on the bench, lowering her gaze from Jody. "I never wanted it to become this way between Maddy and me. It's just that…it seemed like I really didn't have a choice back then."

"I understand," Jody was able to say all too knowingly, "about not having—"

"The judge sent me away," Susan was eager to explain. "Far away from the unfavorable friends I had in Minneapolis to a good rehab center in New York."

"You couldn't make phone calls to your daughter from there?" Elliot made another dig at her, despite Jody's warning.

"I did make some," Susan said. "Not many. I…I'd pretty much come to believe I wasn't fit to be Madison's mother and that it would just be better if I totally dropped out of the picture. *Her* picture."

"No!" Jody emotionally berated the idea.

Susan paused for a moment, first stunned by Jody's outburst, then receptive. "I know now how stupid that was of me. My psychologist, now fiancée, helped me to re-evaluate myself and build a better perspective of my possibilities and responsibilities. When I got out of rehab I got a job and an apartment and, " she slipped a little laugh, "a diamond ring. And then you phoned me out of the blue, Jody."

This woman was counting on a second chance, and Jody knew she couldn't deny her of it. The hard part of it was that before Susan had shown up it had seemed like she was getting her *own* second chance…by way of Mad.

"You've truly been my light, Jody," Susan praised her.

"*Jeez*," Elliot snarled under his breath.

But Jody heard him, recognizing it to mean that he saw her as literally drowning in a fervent involvement with Mad's mother. Which was true. The cards were on the table, Susan had won, and Jody knew her only choice was to allow Susan the chance that she herself ached for.

"She's out back," Jody said, motioning at the door to the break room. The sound of her own voice, giving away Mad's whereabouts, hardly felt like her own. It was like some stranger had entered her mind and was now running the show. Maybe, she thought, the stranger was actually the better side of herself.

Susan stood, giving both Jody and Elliot a look of gratitude before leaving.

When she was gone, Elliot confronted Jody, "*Do you know what you're doing?*"

"Only what I have to."

Together they followed Susan outside.

Chapter 24

When Mad noticed Susan coming toward her in the yard, she froze. But within seconds she smiled as big as any child possibly could and ran to meet her mother with open arms. "Mommy! Mommy, you're here!"

Susan caught her. "Oh, Maddy, my little sunshine… I've missed you so much. But yes, I'm here now, and I love you, sweetie, and we've got so much making up to do."

"I love you too, Mommy. Please don't go away again. Grandma's sick and I don't know what to do about her and—"

"It's gong to be all right now," Susan assured her daughter, stroking her hair and smiling at her with overwhelming happiness. "I'm here to take care of you, Maddy, and of Grandma, too."

"*That's* why Mad didn't want us to call her Maddy," Elliot affirmed to Jody as they sat down on the back steps, keeping their distance from the reunion scene. "It hurt too much for her to hear us call her what her mother had called her."

"Susan really loves her," Jody found it painfully easy to establish. "And there's no doubt that Mad loves Susan."

"Guess kids don't hold grudges. How about you?" Elliot gave her a nudge.

"I probably always will," Jody moaned at the truth of it.

They watched Mad and Susan exchange hugs and giggles on their way out to the shade of the oak tree, where they sat down on the grass to talk.

"Quite a picture, huh?" Elliot remarked.

Jody said nothing, trying to feel nothing.

"Nice, huh?" Elliot kept at her.

"Nice, yes," she answered flatly.

"And it's hurting you like hell, right?"

Jody turned her head to give him a straight look. "What if she still can't be a good mother to Mad?"

"I don't know, but I guess it's out of our hands now. I mean, her coming here like this and planning to marry her—"

"All I know," Jody interrupted, "is that she needs to be forgiven and given a second chance."

Elliot nodded. "The second chance that you never had."

Jody said nothing.

"Reality hits hard, doesn't it."

"I *hate* reality."

He laughed. "I know. But maybe accepting it once and for all can be easier than fighting it."

"You're right," Jody said.

He dipped his head at her. "Try saying it like you mean it."

"I do."

"Come on…" he doubted her.

"Okay, maybe I can't accept my situation," she admitted, "but I can accept theirs, Susan and Mad's."

Elliot dipped his head again, giving her a look off the top of his eyes.

"I'm happy Susan came for her," she said.

"No, you're not."

"I am."

"You're not fooling me, Jody. If you think you can just—"

"Stop it!" she said, already blowing what little composure she thought she'd acquired. "You sympathize with what I'm going through here, and then you tell me to get over it, and when I say that I am you tell me I'm not. What do you expect from me? *What?*"

"I expect you to be honest."

Jody stood up before him, maintaining her eye contact with him from a higher level. "You're a man."

"No kidding."

"Maybe you're the one who doesn't know where real honestly lies in this."

Before either of them could say anything more, Mad noticed them, as if for the first time since she'd noticed her mother's presence, and called out, "Jody! Elliot!"

Mad's exuberant voice knocked Jody's emotional level down still lower. She swallowed the lump in her throat and forced a smile.

Mad came hurrying toward her and Elliot, bringing Susan with by the hand. "My mom's here. She came to get me."

"We know," Jody said. "We've already talked with her."

"It's what I've been praying and praying for," Mad said.

The Way Forward

"Well somebody's been listening, that's for sure," Elliot avowed.

Jody studied the look on Susan's face. It seemed to be a mixture of happiness, guilt, fear, and hope. The same exact feelings she herself was having. She couldn't hate this woman for abandoning her child. Nor could she hate her for coming now to pick up the broken pieces that would grant her a second chance. Jody could see herself in Susan, except for the second chance. For a time Mad seemed to be her second chance. But now, suddenly, she, too, had been snatched away.

"Thank you again, Jody," Susan told her. "For locating me and phoning me. It was exactly the pivotal moment I needed, at exactly the right time, to bring me to my senses."

Jody gave a silent nod.

"I might not be coming over here so much anymore," Mad announced. "I'm going to have a daddy and a big house in New York with my own swing. And Grandma's going to live with us. The daddy I'm getting is a doctor and can help her."

"You're pretty happy, huh?" Elliot broke into a quick grin that failed to hide his sorrow. It wasn't easy for him to let go of this child either.

"I never had a daddy," Mad continued. "Now I'm gonna have my mom and a daddy. And I never been to New York. My mom say's it's nice and it's big. Bigger than Myre."

"*Any* place is bigger than Myre," Elliot quipped.

Jody drew Mad against herself and hugged her tighter than she ever had before. "I'll really, really miss you."

"I'll miss you, too," Mad said in a quivery voice. "But we can write letters."

"Letters," Jody agreed.

"It sounds like you guys have been awfully good to my Maddy," Susan established.

"Awfully," Elliot said, and took his turn to give Mad a hug.

"I'm not sure yet how all this will turn out," Susan admitted, "but—"

"It'll turn out," Jody assured her, "because you and Mad are mother and daughter and that's an unbeatable combination."

Susan was notably touched by Jody's vote of confidence. "Thank you… for so much."

"You're welcome," Jody said, touched as well by the genuineness she'd come to discover in this woman.

"I guess we'll be on our way now," Susan said, taking her daughter's hand. "We've got a lot of things to take care of."

Jody nodded. "I'm sure you have."

"We gotta get ready for New York," Mad said excitedly.

Susan gave Jody and Elliot a last look. "We'll probably see you again before then."

As if that would be enough, Jody thought.

Mad held out her stuffed dog to Jody. "Here, you can have Nips." "No...I can't take him. You'll miss him in New York."

"I want to leave him here with you," Mad insisted needfully.

Jody gave in to the gift that felt like an exchange—Nips for Mad. "Thank you," she managed to tell the child that was slipping out of her life. "I'll love him."

"He'll love you, too," Mad told her. And then as she started away with her mother, she looked back to add, "I love you too, Jody."

The silence left behind by Susan and Mad's departure was deadening. It was the end of the life Jody'd been counting on.

Elliot wrapped his arms around her. He was no doubt himself feeling the pain of this ending. Though Jody felt his heart beating inside his chest, she couldn't feel her own. Surely, at this point, she was dead. *Dead.*

"I'm proud of your bravery," he told her.

"I'm not brave," she said.

"Yes, you are."

"I'm not! I died. Inside I died!"

"Sometimes things have to get worse before they get better."

"Am I there yet?" she asked. "At my worst?"

Elliot laughed lightly. "I think so, yeah."

"So you're saying that now, for my having lost Mad, I'm going to start feeling better?"

He closed his eyes for a moment. "Okay...maybe you're *not* there yet."

Despite feeling dead, Jody was still managing to feel confused. "Whatever you're saying, I'm not getting it."

For a few words his voice was amazingly soft and coaxing. "I'm saying that maybe you have a ways to go yet. I know you're hurting. I know you're angry. But come on, Jody...hit bottom! I mean, really hit your worst. Really get it all out once and for all. *Then* maybe you can move forward."

She gave a reluctant sigh, feeling tired and beat, with no more fight left in her.

From there on Elliot's voice began to rise. "I know that over the years you've carried immense pain and anger over losing your baby. *Jeez*, I know that. But maybe, now, since your experience with Mad, you can recognize that it's time to let it all go once and for all."

"Just like that?" she balked.

"No!" he said. "Not just like that! In a matter of minutes I saw you fold under Susan, going from anger to sympathy. Which is probably as much of a good thing as it is a bad thing, *I don't know.* But I do know that you're not finished with this inside of you yet, are you? There's so much more. And you need to let it out, Jody. All of it. *Jeez.* Scream! Roar at life's unfairness! And the stupid mistakes of youth! Cuss out

The Way Forward

Kevin! Yourself! Your dad! Your brother! And me, if you want! Get it out of your system once and for all, so that maybe...you and me...we can have a fresh start at a real life together. Please... Jody...do this! You can't have your daughter back. I'm sorry, but you can't. You never can. Never!"

Tears spilled from her eyes, while words lay silent in her throat.

"Say something," Elliot urged her.

She didn't.

"It scares the hell out of me when you go silent," he contended.

Jody didn't think there was anything left to say. And if there was, what was the use?

"Come on," he said softly. Then sternly, "*Come on!*"

She turned away from him.

Moving fast and furiously, Elliot stepped around before her and grabbed her by both arms. "Let it go!" he shouted. "Let it go till there's no more left!"

"There's no more left," she said.

"Like hell. You don't think I know you better than that? That this is going to keep eating you forever...unless..."

She tried breaking away from him, but his grip tightened and he started shaking her. He was rough with her, and her head bobbled to and fro, seeming to scramble what little senses she'd had left. *What was he doing to her? How could he be so cruel?*

"It's over!" he said. "You have to face that it's over!"

"I know," she agreed under pressure.

"*Prove* to me that you know. *Prove it!*"

Jody broke free of him by way of letting out a scream so shrill that it ultimately scared him into letting her go. Flailing her hands in the air she cried, "Susan doesn't deserve her!"

"Yeah!" Elliot cheered her on, with a grin of satisfaction spreading across his face. "She certainly had her nerve coming here, right? *Jeez*! Damn her!" He shot his own hands into the air.

"She's Mad's mother and she loves her," Jody reasoned, "and I know how much that's suppose to matter. But I...I can't help feeling left with...with how come *I* never got a second chance?"

"That's so unfair!" Elliot agreed, egging her on.

Jody stuck her hands on her hips. Okay, he'd managed to get her going and she was amazed at finding how good the release felt. She was ready to release some more. "I loved her! I loved my own baby and she just disappeared out of my life within minutes! How could that happen when I didn't want it to happen? I don't understand!"

"Who does?" Elliot said. "Who the hell does? Nobody understands stuff like that. It doesn't mean you have to take it with a lifetime of depression. Purge it once and for all. Do it, Jody!"

"I am."

"Are you more mad than sad?" he asked.

"Yes!"

Elliot coaxed her with an annoying grin. "Show me. You haven't showed me the depth of it yet, have you? Get it all out! Now! Come on! Scream! Shout! Give me hell! Give the world hell! Give God hell! Throw something! Hit something! Let it all go, Jody, because then I want you to get better. For me. For us. I want you to be happy. And free from your past."

"I hate that nurse who walked away with my baby!" she screamed for the whole world to hear. "Her face and her manner…they were so cold!"

"Bad nurse, *bad*," Elliot granted.

"And my Dad!" Jody added. "For ruling over my life the way he did! And Kevin! And Aunt Margo, who—"

"How about God?" Elliot was anxious to ask.

"I don't hate God."

Elliot let out a sigh. "Good."

"But I…I just have so much hate!" she screamed. "And I'm tired of it! I don't want it anymore, Elliot! I don't want it anymore!"

He gave her a calm and tender smile. "It's going, Jody. I can see it leaving you."

She gave him a tearful grin. "Maybe you need glasses."

"I'm not seeing your progress with my eyes, I'm seeing it with my heart."

Half laughing, half crying, she told him, "You…you always try to bring such logic to things."

"One of us has to," he said.

She punched him in the arm. "You don't understand. I don't need logic. Logic's not a cure. It hurts so bad. All the time, it just hurts so bad. Until Mad came along, and then she—"

"She's not your cure, Jody."

"What is? Tell me what is!"

"You yourself, that's your cure. And me…maybe me. Maybe my stupid logic."

She gave him a deep, considering look. Dear, sweet, Elliot. She owed him so much and had only ever taken advantage of his being there. It wasn't right. She needed to start seeing him for his real worth. And maybe, with his help, she'd find the real worth in her own being. "I'm sorry…" she told him.

"For?" he urged her on.

"For needlessly asking you to marry me."

The Way Forward

"*Jeez*, that's right," he quipped. "We no longer have a reason to be married, do we? I wonder if that same guy that hitched us could unhitch us."

Jody studied him, not entirely sure if he was kidding or serious.

He gave her a few moments to wonder. Then he laughed. "Come on… our getting married wasn't needless. At least for me. Marrying you was the best thing I've ever done in my life. If you hadn't asked me, I'd have gotten around to asking you anyway, believe me. And…if there were no Mad in our lives, would you have said yes?"

Now it was she who made *him* wait a few moments, before giving him a smile and a nod.

Elliot pulled her into his arms. "I love you, you crazy girl, and you love me, and that's not at all needless. I think, over time, we've both discovered how much we need each other."

Jody began to feel quiet and calm and sure of things in his embrace. "Logic."

"That's not logic," Elliot told her. "It's love."

"Yeah. I guess."

"You *guess*?"

"I do love you, Elliot."

"You'd better, Mrs. Treggor."

Jody laughed lightly.

"Feeling better now?"

She nodded. "Except…I just…I hope that Susan will really do okay by Mad now. How do we know for sure that she will?"

Elliot grinned. "You forget who she's marrying."

"Her psychologist," Jody said, still finding that funny, despite its solidity.

Elliot's expression became solemn and tender. "You know what, Jody… we can have our own baby. Our very own. Yours and mine. What do you think of that?"

Suddenly it was like sunshine pouring into her heart. "How many?"

Elliot shrugged. "I don't know. A dozen if you want."

"I'd like two."

"Two dozen?" he gasped.

"Two kids."

"Boys or girls?"

"One of each."

He winced. "That could be tricky, but we could put in an order."

Jody smiled demurely.

"You'll be a great mother," he told her.

"And you'll be a great father. I feel like we've learned a lot from Mad, both of us, y'know?"

"A *way* lot. Not just about kids, but about ourselves as well."

She nodded. "I feel like through Mad I've really grown up."

"Well, *finally*!" Elliot exclaimed.

Jody slugged him. Then she said she was sorry. Then Elliot told her to prove it. And then she gave him a very grown-up kiss.

At the end of the day, after Benjamin had arrived for the night shift, Jody and Elliot strolled hand-in-hand down the wooded path to their cottage.

"Thank you for being you," she told her husband, freshly taking in the very fact that he *was* her husband.

"You're welcome. And thank you for being you."

Jody gave a long sigh. "After everything…I'm feeling more like me now than I have in a long time."

"Welcome to the real world, Mrs. Treggor."

"*Our* world," she corrected him.

"It's gonna be good, Jody."

"I know," she said.

They smiled at each other, and Elliot squeezed her hand, verifying, "Two kids?"

"A boy and a girl," she said.

"Right." He leaned over to kiss her cheek.

"Well, not that *way* will we have them," she teased.

Elliot stopped walking, pulled her swiftly into his arms, and gave her a long passionate kiss.

"Not that way either," Jody laughed, taking off into a run ahead of him.

"Hey, you crazy girl!" he called, coming after her. "I'm not stupid, you know!"

"Prove it," she said, entering the front door of the cottage.

"Exactly my intent." He followed her inside, letting the door slam shut behind him.

Jody giggled.

Elliot laughed.

Then the cottage turned blissfully quiet.

The End

Marilyn DeMars may be contacted by e-mail lardem@usfamily.net

NORMANDALE COMMUNITY COLLEGE
LIBRARY
9700 FRANCE AVENUE SOUTH
BLOOMINGTON, MN 55431-4399